SUDDEN VIOLENCE

Violet was warm, godawful warm. She and Shelter lay panting beneath the blankets, the rain washing down with gentle warmth. He felt her lips against his, the softness of her flesh and then a sudden violence.

The blankets were drawn tight around them, hands grabbed hold of Shelter's shoulders and a fist slammed against the side of his skull. He tried to struggle, but the blankets were like a cocoon. He and Violet were rolled over twice, and then Shelter felt the sharp binding of ropes.

"Now ain't that a pretty package for ye," Jethro Partridge said with a vicious grin.

"What do you want, Jethro?"

"I want the girl, and then I want that damned gold cache of your'n." He stood and eared back the hammer of his rifle. "And you're takin' me to it or you'll never take anyone anywhere again!"

#7

SHELTER

LOOKOUT MOUNTAIN

BY
PAUL LEDD

ZEBRA BOOKS

KENSINGTON PUBLISHING CORP.

ZEBRA BOOKS

are published by

KENSINGTON PUBLISHING CORP.
21 East 40th Street
New York, N. Y. 10016

Printed in the United States of America

1.

The cannon flashed in the night and flame erupted, scorching the silence as the gray webbing of sleep was shattered by the roar of the guns. Shelter rolled, grabbed for his Colt and blinked the night away. He was naked, sweating, cold. The room tilted slightly for a moment before he got his bearings, sweeping away the last, bloody cobwebs of his dream.

That endless dream still haunted him. Endless as the war itself had been endless. As this

5

mad bloody chase was endless. Shelter swung his feet to the cold hardwood floor, biinking at the yellow-orange light which seeped through the window shade of the hotel room.

He rose, naked still, the Colt still in his hand, lingering like a cold, explosive memory. He walked to the window and raised the shade. The sun flooded away the last fragments of memory.

He leaned on the sill and stared down at the street, a tall, night-tousled lean man with dark, unbarbered hair and icy blue eyes which measured the city.

In New Orleans you can hear music in the morning.

A brassy racketing preceded a small parade. Five people, one a woman. They had a tuba, a fiddle, a cornet and a banjo. The woman, wearing a black dress and a formless black hat, rattled a tambourine as they marched slowly through the French Quarter. Returning from or going to an early morning funeral, it seemed. The woman's black face was swollen with grief. The music seemed to exorcise her pain, and with each step she banged the tambourine against her heavy thigh, driving the demons out of her tormented body.

The sheets rustled softly behind him and he heard the footsteps glide across the floor toward him. Her soft lips touched his shoulder and her dark, silky hair spilled across his back.

"What was it?" Elizabeth asked.

"Nothing. A small parade."

6

"And that woke you?" she asked.

"No." Shelter turned to her, folding her warmth in his arms. She was not vulnerable in her nakedness, but proud, like some ancient savage princess. Her eyes sparked with warmth and with desire as she pressed her lips against his, tasting his taste, teasing his lower lip, her breasts warm against Shelter's bare chest.

She was supple, quite strong beneath the layer of woman fat. Her breasts held firmly when she moved; her legs were straight, smoothly muscular.

She smelled now of the night. Her dark hair twisted and formed by night fingers. She swayed against him, and he held her tightly.

"I nearly fainted," she admitted with a surprised laugh.

"Shelter, the lady killer," he replied, kissing her eyelids.

"Yes." Her gaze went steamy. "At least you've damn sure wounded a few, Shelter Morgan."

Her eyes met his cool blue eyes. She let her fingers roam across his broad shoulders, down the tanned sinew of his arms. She tilted her head forward and kissed his chest.

Outside the black wrought iron balconies overhung the brick street. The leaves on the trees shimmered like new doubloons in the early morning light. Elizabeth's eyes shimmered with an equally bright glow. He led her to the bed and she sat, leaning back slowly as he fell to join her, his mouth searching her body,

7

tasting the salt and cinnamon of her breasts, her soft, flat stomach. Her breasts rose and fell and his lips tasted the taut, eager nipples which blossomed there, growing to his lips from out of the wide, dark aureolas.

She was tiger strength and woman warmth beneath him, her breath misting against his ear, her hands like kitten paws smooth against his growing erection. She positioned him, her thighs spreading. Then he felt the swollen head of his shaft meet the summery dew of her and slip inside like a fevered, throbbing mouse into its accustomed refuge.

"That's good," she whispered to him. "Very deep and warm and there . . ." her voice broke off, "did you feel that . . . when it scrapes at my flesh." She swayed and trembled. "Like untying all the nerves, laying me bare." She smiled. "No pun."

She was sweet and savage, a misty rain forest, a humid thrumming, a rolling ship traversing a joyous, emotion-tossed sea. Her body responded to his, fitting every contour perfectly. Her throat was soft, trembling beneath his lips. Her mouth was slack, hungry.

He got to his knees unsteadily, letting his hands rest on her hip bones as his thumbs tangled themselves in her soft, curly nest between her thighs as his cock slid and swelled within her, a hungry crimson, glossed with her honey.

He eased even closer, wanting to go through her, to cleft her, to let her devour him. Her hands joined his, their fingers commingled, tracing patterns across her clitoris and lingering on his shaft. Her eyes were distant, so full of enjoyment that she appeared to be in pain.

The tendons in her neck were taut. Her thigh muscles rippled with effort as they neared a breaking point, a wonderful exchange, a partnership in heated joy.

"Shelter. It's good. It's coming, here . . . " she stretched her hands toward his shoulders and he pressed himself against her fervent, heated body, feeling the tide change within her, the rolling ebb and flow becoming a raging, irresistible rip current which pummeled her, drowning her as it dragged her out of herself, exploding seaward in a cascade of white water froth. She felt herself going down, drowning, her nails digging at Shell's shoulders, her eyes going wide with alarm . . . and then she smiled, sinking to the sensation-flooded depths.

"Shelter. Again, damn you." She smiled, a wistful, dreamy smile. "You did it again. So nice. So bright — I see the lights on a summer lake, brilliant sunlight. Prickles of sensation . . . oh, God!" she growled suddenly as she discovered the current had not died away, but had dropped her only to circle like a tormenting, devouring shark and she shuddered, her body racing to swim ahead of the second rush of joy, her hips thrashing, her heart pounding as Shelter filled her with the awesome, savage happiness of primitive awareness.

She saw his face tense, lifted her head to

see his erection disappear into her downy bush and she stretched out a hand to feel it, to know it. He slid through her fingers, into her womb, into her hot secret recesses. She clutched at him, cradling his taut scrotum, wanting him to fill her with more of the sea's raging joy, to lift her on a crest of watery need and slam her down into the depths of fulfillment.

He tensed, and she felt a change in him, felt a driving need begin to build and she encouraged him, her hands drifting across his hips, touching the smooth flesh of his taut buttocks, stroking his massive, violent and gentle cock.

"Push," Elizabeth breathed. "Push me over the edge. Push again." And his pelvis ground against hers, his sinews and strapping muscle flexed, his arteries swollen with desire, his eyes fixed on hers as she felt his last thrust, felt him finish with a driving stroke which drove the breath out of her and caused a humid, brilliant flower to blossom deep with her.

Shelter came with a shuddering, loin-muffled explosion and he felt her body drink greedily of his. He felt the riptide then as well, felt it swell, break, threaten to draw him out of himself and into her dark, welcoming sea-cavern.

He lay against Elizabeth, touching her throat, her tiny copper ear, smelling the spices of her body, his heart stilling and he gave it thought: this could be the one. By God, she could be the one to cause him to give it up, the thunder of the guns, the pain, the boiling blood, the agony of shattered bones and torn flesh.

Beautiful she was, and knowing. Easy to talk to, difficult to leave.

Elizabeth Townshend made life too sweet to lose. She stroked his back with her palm, humming a soft tune deep in her throat. She noticed his silence, and she asked, "What is it, Shell? Still thinking about Roland Blue?"

"Not about him. About the others. The other Roland Blues, the other murderers. Blue we don't have to think about. He's dead in Mexico, and he didn't deserve to go so easily."

Elizabeth scooted up and leaned against the headboard, watching the mockingbird peering in their sunbright window. Far off a steamboat whistle sounded, reminding her of their first meeting.

"You should just let the thoughts go," she said gently. "Shrug them off."

"I know what I *should* do," Shelter said with a flicker of a smile. "But they're ghost riding me, Liz. Mean old bloody ghosts. Men who killed friends of mine, killed boys I never did know but who fought with me."

"I know, you told me."

"Yes. More than once." He smiled again. He had told her everything, but things like that can't be told properly, the horror of it all, the blood and tumble of it. Closing his eyes for only a moment, Shelter drifted back through the blue smoke of time.

11

He was up from Tennessee, and when the Confederacy called, he enlisted, a long-geared, barefoot kid who got his first pair of new boots ever from the quarter-master along with a slow, deadly muzzle loader. He had fought beside Stonewall Jackson before Jackson went down, and found his senses heightened by battle flame, smothered by blood and agonized screams. It was a mad scramble for survival, and Shelter Morgan had been born a-scramblin'. He survived, enduring the slush and ice, the storms of cannon balls, the privation and hunger.

During that last bootless, grubless year there wasn't a man fighting for the gray that didn't know they were whipped, but they fought on. It was duty and they stuck with it. It was a dismal, smoke-filled, icy year, a year in which they curled their tails under their legs and slunk steadily backward, withdrawing into Georgia to sag to the charred earth.

Unexpectedly a little glimmer of hope pierced the war clouds in Georg..., there along the bloody Conasauga River. "Captain Morgan?"

Captain Shelter Morgan glanced up from beneath the brim of his hat. He had been resting war-weary muscles in the dusty shade of a cannon-struck white oak. He lifted red-rimmed, weary eyes to the man standing over him. His eyelids moved across his eyes as if they were studded with jagged glass.

"What is it, Chambers?" Shelter asked.

"The colonel wants to see you, sir."

"We moving again?"

"I couldn't say, Captain, you'd have to ask the colonel."

"All right." Shelter came to his feet, grunting with the exertion. His weary muscles had locked on him as they cooled. He followed Chambers back to Captain Fainer's tent, dusting his battle shredded uniform as well as possible as they walked through the soldiers who slumped against the earth, sleeping the sleep of the weary and of the dead.

From the surgeon's table a man shrieked — a terrible, pain flooded cry for mercy. And then the cry broke off, death having brought mercy.

They had no morphine, they had no bandages, as they had no food no ammunition and no blankets. Snow patched a small area beside the colonel's tent. Shelter frowned.

There were six horses tied up beside the frame and canvas of the tent. All sleek, healthy animals, unfamiliar to Morgan. He rapped on the tent frame and was summoned.

They sat around the makeshift table, six officers of whom Shelter knew four. Two other men stood in the shadows which cobwebbed the corner of Fainer's tent. A blade of light flashed on the epaulet one of them wore. The insignia of a general officer glittered in that light.

Fainer rose to meet Shell. "Sit down son. Sit down. You know most everyone — Wakefield, Twyner, Bowlen."

Yes, he knew them. Wakefield, the former

plantation owner, the sharp-edged aristocrat who even now wore a spotless uniform; Twyner, who had lost an arm and was immersed now in his own pool of bitterness. Bowlen who had an easy smile and a trunk full of hoarded tinned goods.

Major Benton Gray was there as well, a damned good line officer with a flair for mounted combat and a thin scar running through his eye the length of his face. The general stepped forward and Shelter was introduced.

"Shelter, this is General Custis. General, Captain Morgan."

"So this is the man," Custis said. He nodded, his green eyes expressionless as he surveyed Shelter Morgan.

Shelter shot a glance at Colonel Fainer but Fainer only nodded as if to say—it's all right. Shell shrugged, pulled up a barrel and sat down. Wakefield didn't like it much when Shelter sat next to him.

Wakefield felt himself a patrician, born to command, to wear rank. Morgan had enlisted, and his rank was a battlefield commission earned under Jackson as they all knew. Wakefield sniffed slightly and looked with hooded eyes at Morgan.

Shelter could shrug all of that off. Wakefield was the only officer who affected disdain. Fainer was his commanding officer, and a damn good friend. He didn't know Gray well, since he was cavalry, but he had a reputation for bravery and for suffering with and for his men.

"Well?" Shelter asked finally. There was a decision being made; behind those green eyes of General Custis the wheels spun. Eventually he nodded.

"I understand you're up from Tennessee, Morgan," the general said, puffing tenderly on a cigar.

"I am sir, from near to Chickamauga. Pikeville the town is called."

"In the very shadow of Lookout Mountain."

"Just about, General."

"To you then Chickamauga is a good place, a familiar hearth." General Custis sighed audibly. "To me, Captain, it is a flaming memory. We got our butts whipped up there."

"You were with Bragg, sir?"

"I was." The general was silent a moment, rocking on his heels, puffing his cigar, hands behind his back. "Chickamauga was the turning point, Captain. We had crested the mountain, and then by God the Yankees came and shoved us down the far side. We might have lost it all right there, Captain."

From across the camp another scream sounded. It flitted into the tent and lingered there like a bitter, haunting memory.

"You heard that?" Custis asked.

"That one and many more." What else was there to hear after the guns, when the surgery was done with a meat saw, when there was no morphine, when the wounds were cauterized, the blood vessels sealed off by a red hot iron applied to raw meat?

"Do you want to stop it, Captain Morgan?"

Shelter's eyes narrowed, not getting the man's point. "Sir?"

"That and the amputated, frostbitten toes and fingers. That and the gnawing hunger, the dysentery—which has undoubtedly killed more of our soldiers than all the enemy musket balls."

"Some of those people are mine," Shelter answered. "My boys. I led them into that pain. You're damned right I want to lead them out of it. Now suppose you stop beating around the bush and tell me what in hell you're talking about . . . Sir," he added.

Custis smiled faintly. He was a handsome man with curled silver hair and an officer's erect carriage. Lines of humor rayed out from around his eyes. Now they deepened as he grunted and studied Shelter Morgan afresh.

"You put it on the line, don't you, Morgan?"

"There's not much time to waste, sir. You yourself said that. If there's a job to be done, let's get to it. If I'm your man—I assume that's what you're deciding right now."

"It's decided," Custis said. "You're my man. Now listen to what I'm going to say.

"When Sherman pushed General Bragg out of Tennessee we left a lot behind. We broke and ran, Captain. Plain ran. There's something we left behind which could help us now."

"Cannon?"

16

Custis's eyes narrowed. "No, Morgan. Gold. A quarter of a million dollars in gold."

Shelter whistled and Custis went on. "That gold was supposed to be delivered through to Virginia to General Lee, but the couriers were cut off. They took refuge with Bragg near to Lookout Mountain. When we retreated there was no time to carry anything but our skins, Captain."

"The gold is still there."

"It is." Custis glanced at Fainer. "The colonel has confidence in you, Captain. In your courage and loyalty. I want to know if you can break out of Georgia and get back to Chickamauga and recover that gold. A lot depends on it, son, a lot."

"There's a hundred thousand men around us, sir." Shelter was silent, thinking of that country, the deep blue-gray haze drifting over the scarlet and gold autumn colored trees, the cold, quick creeks and deeply shaded valleys.

He said, "Maybe. With only a handful of men. Just enough to carry the gold—if you can mark the spot on the map. Maybe. If we keep to the high ridges, moving only at night. Maybe."

"Just maybe?" Wakefield said stiffly.

"That's all I can promise, Gordon," Shelter answered. "Perhaps you'd like to volunteer for this assignment?"

"Men." Fainer's voice was calming, firm.

"I'll give it my best, sir," Shelter said. "I want to pick my own men. Those I know best."

17

"Of course, Captain," Custis agreed. "I can't overemphasize the importance of this mission. We've boys dying in pain with no morphine to smother it. We've boys who are going to freeze this winter. Many of them. We're fighting repeating rifles with muzzle loaders. With no money to buy new weapons from our sources.

"There's another aspect I haven't mentioned," Custis went on. "We must fight on as long as possible. For that we need supplies. If we can't mount new offensives and are forced to surrender poorly, unconditionally, we will never see the South again as we knew it.

"A negotiated peace out of strength is our only hope now. We all know . . . it's coming to the last hour. But if it has to be unconditional, if we have no arms to lay down, no threats to hold over Grant's head, then the South will be buried, stripped, plundered and raped. There won't be seed for crops, houses for our families, food for the babies."

Wakefield came suddenly alert as the general spoke in this vein. Shelter knew why. The man expected to return to his plantation, had every hope of living as he always had. Yet Shelter was thinking of the other things—the screams of pain still rang in his ears. He had seen his men freeze to death already. He wanted to see no more of it.

"I'll give it hell," he promised. "That's all I can promise."

"That's all we can ask, Morgan. All we can expect."

18

When Shelter was gone, his gray clad figure striding through the camp, Custis turned to Colonel Fainer. "I hope we haven't made a mistake, Colonel. That's a lot of money, a lot of trust to drop in one man's lap."

"Captain Morgan's the man for it, sir," Fainer said, turning from the tent flap. "He's got the courage, the devotion to duty. He knows the area. He's our man, sir. Besides," he shrugged, "who else is there? Whatever hope have we got otherwise?"

Shelter picked his men: Keane who was the marksman; Dinkum who could scrounge a living from the scorched countryside better than any Indian Shelter had met; Welton Williams, a cold hawk-faced man who could do things with a pistol other men only dreamed of; and Sergeant Jeb Thornton.

Wearing civilian clothes, riding horses with the CSA brands blurred, they rode out at nightfall, the soft moon drifting through a smoky night.

Incredibly they made it back. Keane was picked off by a Union sharpshooter when he carelessly skylined himself. Thornton had been wounded, but he would make it. The pack horses waddled under the weight of their burden.

Sherman was still pressing forward. Fainer had withdrawn again, leaving only a row of new graves to mark the old camp. "Now what?" Welton Williams had asked sourly. "You know, Cap, we're likely not to find him. And despite

19

what Custis and them say, we've lost and this gold ain't going to win it for us."

"What are you suggesting, Welton?" Jeb Thornton asked. The big man glowered at the wolfish Welton Williams.

"Just what you think I'm suggesting," Williams said, pausing to spit. "Say we can deliver this gold. There's no way to exchange it for guns, for food. Not quick enough. We'd just be turning it over to the Union, more'n likely. We fought for this gold. We got as much right to it as anybody."

"No." Captain Shelter Morgan's blue eyes were cold. Fire and ice. Welton Williams was a gun hawk, but even he shifted his gaze a little under those eyes. "We're soldiers, Williams. By God, until Lee surrenders I'm doing what I took an oath to do. Maybe it's not smart, but it's right."

"Duty!" Welton scoffed.

"That's right. I'm not throwing away my reputation, my dignity, for that gold. A man without dignity, he isn't much, Williams. And mine can't be bought."

They rode on silently, the horses stirring the ash underfoot. The sun blinked through the blackened, wrought iron tree limbs. He was there suddenly, ahead of them. A man in civilian clothes and Welton Williams brought up his two Smith & Wesson pistols before any of them could so much as blink the hammers eared back, ready to fire.

"Don't shoot! For God's sake." The man

20

threw down his rifle. "Captain Morgan?" he asked.

"That's right." Shelter eased his horse forward. Welton Williams' guns hadn't wavered.

"I was posted on this road to watch for you, sir. To take you to Colonel Fainer's new position."

Shelter was cautious. "What the hell happened to your uniform, mister?"

"Colonel thought it'd be better for his scouts to go civilian, Captain."

"Sir," Jeb Thornton volunteered, "it's all right. I recognize him now. He's out of Major Twyner's staff."

"All right." Shelter glanced at Welton who holstered his guns. "Lead on then," Shell told the man. "Slowly."

"Yes, sir."

They rode through the blackened countryside, winding up to a high crest where the oaks ringed a grassy meadow. Shelter saw them come slowly out of the trees.

Twenty men, all known to him, all in civilian clothes. Colonel Fainer rode to him dressed in an immaculate white suite, white planter's hat.

"You made it, Shell. Good boy!"

"What the hell is this, Colonel?" Shell asked. The men flanking Fainer were armed, rifles across the saddlebows. The colonel smiled uncertainly.

"Why it's only us, Captain."

"You know what I mean. Why the civilian

21

clothes? Someone sign an armistice?"

General Custis was beyond Fainer, sitting a fine black Tennessee Walker. Beside him a sergeant named Plum, another named Whistler.

Shell looked them over, remembering their names, their faces which glittered with gold lust. He knew already, knew and he felt his heart go cold.

"It's the gold, Shell. You must have guessed. Turn it over."

"I can't, sir."

"Be reasonable, Shell. The war's over. We all know that. And what are we going home to? What do we have to show for our effort, our wounds? Burned fields, requisitioned houses, nothing!" He ran a hand nervously across his brow. "Damn it, Shelter, we deserve something. A chance to start again somewhere else. The gold can give us that. Give it to your men as well."

Dinkum was rigid in his saddle, Jeb Thornton was curled up with pain. Welton's horse's hooves whispered against the grass.

"We ain't going to get out of here no way, sir," Williams said in a low voice.

Shelter knew it was true. He looked into Fainer's eyes, into the eyes of a man he had respected and trusted. He saw Fainer reach up and scratch his ear.

Whether that had been the signal or not Shelter never knew, but he saw a man's rifle come around, heard the thunder of Welton Williams' twin pistols, saw a face explode into a mask of blood, heard the scream of pain from Dink's lips.

He felt a branding iron plunged into his leg, felt the hot blood surge out. Then Shelter was firing, the gunsmoke drifting past them as Welton Williams, punctured by bullets, dropped to the cold earth as Jeb fell.

"Run, damnit!" he hollered at Dinkum. The soldier, dazed behind his spectacles, heeled his horse hard and he plunged off into the brush, Shelter covering his retreat as the pain swirled up and filled his gut with nausea, his head with hot dizziness.

The guns roared and he fired until his pistol was empty. Then he rode, pain riding with him, through the thickening shadows. They rode behind him, their angry swarm of bullets chopping at the brush around him.

He made the river, finding Dinkum dead at its edge. Then he let his horse run and fell to the earth, staggering into the brush as the night came on, as his knees buckled and went to rubber.

He dragged himself into a thicket where he sat trying desperately to reload, to stem the flow of blood. He sat panting, fevered, his Colt cradled in his hand.

The dazed hours swam past. The moon floated high. They did not come, and then they were around him. Shell saw lanterns flashing along the Conasauga and he drew back the hammer of his Colt with both thumbs, lifting it shakily.

23

They burst into the thicket then, guns levelled. He hadn't even the strength to lift his gun.

"Drop it, Johnny! It's all over."

Shelter saw the lanternlight on their blue uniforms, saw the Union soldier reach down cautiously and lift his gun from his dead hand. He stared at them and then began to laugh, laugh until the wound in his side exploded with pain and the night, the moon, the soldiers spun away in a brilliant spiral and the world went suddenly dark and silent.

2.

The morning sun was brilliant, warm on
Shelter's shoulders though Bourbon Street
was still deep in shadow. A beer wagon clattered
by and Shelter sipped at his coffee, watching
as Elizabeth, across the white metal table,
finished her toast with small, thoughtful bites.

The sun burnished her dark hair, shadowing
her elegant features. She felt his eyes on her
and blinked. "Still thinking?"

"Of this and that."

"Not of the war."

"Yes," he had to admit. "That and all that's come after."

"And of me?" she asked.

"Just a little," Shelter answered.

She smiled, toyed with her food and then said, "They imprisoned you, didn't they? As a spy."

"Since I was captured in civilian clothes, yes."

"But no one would listen to your story about the massacre and the gold."

Shell leaned back in his chair. "No. There wasn't must interest in it. No proof. I was the only living witness and we were all Confederates. The men had scattered, all moving west, it seems, where they weren't known. Some took new names. Most of them stayed with crime."

"Like Roland Blue."

"Yes. Some were worse than him."

She shuddered at the thought. Together Shelter and Elizabeth had finished off Blue and his gun smuggling ring. The government had sent her down to play a part in a confidence game, a part she had performed so well she had Shelter duped.

"How many have there been, Shell? How many are left?"

"You want to see the list?"

"I've seen it. It scares me." She was silent a time, watching the sun creep out onto Bourbon Street as the waiter in a white coat poured them more coffee.

How many. So many. Too many. Wakefield, Mason, Twyner, Captain Bowlen, Chambers, Plum, Fainer and Custis. Hugh Whistler who turned out to be innocent but who died anyway, Welton Williams who died twice, and all of the others, men caught in the swirl of things, events which dragged them down.

It was a sorry slate. But not as sorry as the list Shelter did not keep—that which would be the roll of those who had died in pain, frozen or starved because their officers, their friends had betrayed them.

That was what kept him going. That scream of pain which would never stop echoing in his ears.

How many more? He mentally scanned the list. Ten down, ten to go. Benton Gray, Joshua Pickett, who was supposed to be in Dakota Territory . . . Shelter rubbed his eyes. Looking up he saw her sweet concern. Her hand came across the table, touching his.

"You could let it lie. The longer this goes on . . . I've seen the scars you already carry on your body. There will be another bullet, Shell. The last one."

"I know. Maybe . . . "

He noticed from the tail of his eye a tall, raggedly dressed man, hat in hands. The kid was standing agape, eyes pinned on Shelter Morgan, jaw slack. Somehow he seemed familiar and Shelter frowned.

Elizabeth's head turned as well and she saw the man take a halting step toward them. She

27

noticed his worn tweed coat, the homespun pants, the oversized, scuffed shoes. But there was something about him. Maybe the eyes.

He came over, squinting into the sun, his gaze fixed on Shell. Finally he gave a loud whoop and slapped his hat on his thigh.

"I'll be wrung and dried! Shelter Morgan. I'll be go to hell and gone if it ain't Shelter be-damned Morgan!"

He spun a white wire chair around and straddled it. He flung his elbows up on the table and sat there grinning.

"Do I know you?" Shell asked.

"Hell, yes. Though it was a time before I recognized you in them fancy clothes. Here in New Orleans. Ain't that a sharp kick! Shelter Morgan." He smiled at Elizabeth.

"And you are?" Shell prompted.

"Duncan Corbett! Old Duncan Corbett, cousin. Kinfolk from Tennessee. Don't tell me you been gone so long you cain't remember old Duncan? We used to fish Gaines Crick up past the falls, hoot and holler and brawl at the Sunday Socials. Tell me I'm lyin'," he said with a smile and a wink.

"Dunc!" Shelter peered at the kid. "You've grown two feet. Elizabeth, this gangling hillbilly is telling the truth. Uncle Josiah Morgan married up to a Kincaid and one of those fool Kincaid girls married a Corbett. Duncan is their get."

Elizabeth smiled, noticing that Shelter had drifted into long-forgotten speech patterns.

28

She shook the rough red hand of Duncan Corbett and smiled. "You two must want to talk," she said.

"You stay and set," Duncan said. "A pretty woman sweetens the air and brightens the conversation, ain't that right, Shell?"

"The Morgan tongue, I see," Elizabeth said, glancing at Shelter.

"Thank you, Ma'm," Duncan said, "but if I ever had the tongue of *that* Morgan, I'd be knee deep in grass widows. I mind a time . . ."

"Dunc." Shell discouraged him.

"Why, you're right. Excuse me, Ma'm. You likely wouldn't be admiring of Shell's old ways."

"It might be intriguing," Elizabeth said. Her eyes smiled. She rested her chin on her hands, gazing at Shelter. "But perhaps it's best if I don't know."

"Mebbe," Dunc said considering it. "What in hell are you doin' in New Orleans, Shell?"

"Just travelling through. How about you?"

Shelter lifted his cup, finished his coffee and watched Duncan's sharply angled face which now was drawn with seriousness.

"Come lookin' for Tom and Bob Partridge, Shelter. They're cousins too, Ma'm," he told Elizabeth. "But I might have got luckier finding you. We need your gun, Shelter," Duncan said

Elizabeth felt her heart contract and turn over. She glanced quickly at Shell whose expression had not changed.

"My gun?" he repeated.

29

"Yes sir, your gun." Duncan hunched closer. "It's all opened up again, Shell. Polly Partridge she got pregnant — 'scuse me, Ma'm — by Aaron Plank. Then Jethro, Polly's pa went stalkin' and shot Aaron dead. Then it come to a head again, Shelter. The feud is on."

"Feud?" Elizabeth frowned at Shelter.

"The Planks and the Morgan-Corbetts have been feuding in those hills for two hundred years, Elizabeth. They say they both came over on the same ship and it started there. Hell, there's nobody living who remembers what started it. I recall a lot of it as a boy. A Morgan sniped at, a Plank burned out."

"Sure you recall," Duncan said with animation. "And as soon as I saw you I knew you were the man for it. I knowed you'd want to revenge Polly."

"Dunc," Shell said wearily, "I don't want to revenge Polly Partridge or any of the others who have been killed senselessly. The feud is a relic of a savage past, and it ought to be stopped."

"Sure, sure," Duncan agreed. "And you're the man to stop it."

"No. I'm not the man for that. I have roots in those hills, but they've all been torn loose. I don't have the urge to seek vengeance for a girl I hardly know, blood ties or none. I don't have the urge to watch whole families killed off. And it has happened, and will again."

"I don't get you, Shell," Dunc said with bewilderment.

30

"I've been gone a long time, Dunc. I never did think that feuding was much of an idea. That's as simple as I can put it. Let the law take care of things."

"Ain't no law," Dunc said, tilting back. " 'Cept for Constable Rains, and he's . . . "

"I know. He's a Plank."

"Right." Duncan's puzzled eyes studied Shelter. "Anyway," he mumbled, "Rains has gone on down to Nashville, hopin' Senator Gray can get him an appointment to the State Police . . . "

"Gray?" Shelter's head came around.

"Benton Gray. State Senator Gray. He's got him a house up near us, spends most of his time there, but they was having a special session in Nashville and so Benton . . . "

"Benton Gray," Shelter repeated.

"That's what I said, ain't it?"

"A tall man with a hawk nose, thinning hair. Moves with a limp."

"Sure. That's Benton Gray to a tee. You met up with him, Shelter?"

"Yes. I've met up with him. Long ago. In Georgia."

Gray had been an officer Shelter respected and liked. Up until the moment he had seen Gray in that clearing, sitting a leggy roan, gun in his hand, a cool smile on his lips. Until Benton Gray opened up with that pistol, spilling Jeb Thornton from his saddle as calmly as if he were potting game.

"I recall him," Shelter said. "Look Dunc,

31

where are you staying? I'll think this over and get in touch with you."

"You've changed your mind!" Duncan was jubilant.

"Maybe. Maybe so."

"Great shakes! Now we can't lose." He rose. "Look, Shell, I'm in a place called Cotton House down on the docks. I'll be there or leave a note. I've still got to find Tom and Bob Partridge. They flat-boated on down and ain't even heard about this. When they do — those boys will be fightin' mean. Then the four of us, we'll clean up this Plank trouble in two shakes of a lamb's tail."

"Sure, Dunc. I'll think about it, all right."

When Duncan was gone Elizabeth asked, "Who is Benton Gray, Shelter?"

"One of them," he answered.

"That's what I was afraid of. So you'll go," she said, looking at her hands and not at him.

"I'll think of it."

"You know I don't want you to go."

"I know that, Liz. God, you should know that I don't want to either."

"But you will," she said with resignation. She rose and he stood, dabbing at his mouth with the napkin.

"I'll think on it."

They wound their arms around each other's waists and walked back to their room, moving through a haze which seemed to have settled between them. Their perfect moment was already drifting away.

When Shelter came back from the bath down the hall Elizabeth was standing at the window, wearing a white silk wrapper. She turned, smiling inscrutably. She let her wrapper part.

"We should say goodbye properly."

"I didn't think that was decided. Are we saying goodbye?"

Shelter sat on the bed, tossing his robe aside. She came to him, her hand resting on his naked, muscle-woven thigh.

She let her head rest against his thigh while her hand hefted the sack which hung between his legs. Gently her fingers roamed up his shaft, her fingernails inscribing the lightest floral patterns around the tip of it. He patted her head, running his fingers through her sleek, dark hair. Her hair spilled across his thigh, brushed his scrotum. Her eyes were bright as her finger traced the veins on his shaft. Her breath was against his flesh, stimulating, moist.

"Don't go, Shelter," she said in a murmur.

He lifted her face to his, kissed her deeply, letting her darting tongue shimmy between his lips. Then he lay her back, his hands going to her hips to draw her astride as he rolled to his back.

She was flooding with emotion, and she positioned herself quickly, impaling herself on his thick cock, settling with a sigh, a catching of her breath. Her hair swept across his abdomen as she swayed to a silent, pagan rhythm.

Shelter's hands ran along the silky contours of her hips, and he cupped her swaying breasts as she worked herself against him, rising and settling with tiny expulsions of breath, her face a study of concentration as she used the friction of their bodies to spark the tinder deep within her.

It caught fire, held and burst into devouring flame as Shelter watched. Her face went alternately taut and slack, her mouth hung open. She touched her tongue to her dry lips, her hips rolling and jerking as she flexed against him, drawing him into the flames, building an insistent need in his loins.

Shelter arched his back, thrust out. Thrust again, feeling her quivering, satin flesh grasp at his, demand of it, nibble and then snap at it, and he came in a driving rush, feeling her come as well, her body shaken like that of a dervish in the throes of religious ecstasy.

She was warm against him, soft. The day was a cooling, gentle time. They spoke and touched, exchanging small kisses. They spoke of what they would do, what they would like to do.

Shelter told her of an island he knew far away where there was no need for clothing, for working to produce the necessities of life. Fruit hung heavy from the glossy trees, fish swam gill to gill in the cove. There was a waterfall, an unchanging idyllic climate.

They spoke of that, of many things far distant in time and place. And now and then of duty. Elizabeth was long overdue in Washington and Shelter had the scent of a bloody trail.

They changed the topic whenever it drifted to duty, speaking of soft dreams, whimsical wishes. Elizabeth was forlorn when Shelter spoke of Gray, of Tennessee, and she begged him to leave it alone, knowing that he could not.

In the end she too had to bow to duty, and they clung together on the steamboat dock, the stacks of white smoke flooding the clear blue Gulf skies. Then the brassy whistle blew. Once, twice. They clung together, separated and then clung again to each other, murmuring, promising empty promises.

And then she was gone, a silent figure in white against the rail as the paddle wheeler muddled up the long lazy Mississippi, as the tall dark man watched it make the bend in the river, then turned and strode uptown, toward the Cotton House.

Duncan Corbett answered the door in shirt-sleeves, swung it wide, grinning, clasping Shelter's hand and babbling.

"Damn, Shell, glad to see you. Knew you'd come. Knew you wouldn't let the clan down."

The two dark eyed men with surly expressions, matching fly-away black hair slumped on the bed, eyeing Shelter with frank appraisal.

"Boys, you recall Shelter Morgan. A Pikeville Morgan. Shell, these are Tom and Bob Partridge, grown some since you saw them last, I'd bet."

"Boys," Shelter nodded. No one made a move to shake hands. The Partridge boys had that surliness common in the hills, their protection from outsiders, hated flatlanders, the educated. Shelter was not one of them. He had been, but he had left the hills and was now tainted by the flatlanders himself.

"Morgan . . ." Tom Partridge was thoughtful. His dark eyes brightened. "Ain't he the one . . . ?"

"Shut up, Tom!" his brother snapped. Shelter glanced from one to the other.

"The one who what?" he inquired.

Bob spoke for his brother. "He was thinkin' you were the one who shot Dance Plank. He knows it ain't polite to speak out and tell who done what back up in the hills."

It was a totally unconvincing explanation, but Shelter let it lie. Dance Plank, as he remembered, had been ambushed years ago by old Frank Lee Partridge. Shelter had never killed a man before the war. He had learned respect for life from his father, an outcast of sorts since he too refused to take part in the feud.

"The boys and me was just talkin'," Duncan Corbett said, sitting on the sagging bed himself. "We're meaning to ride back up. They come down on a flatboat, and it's too damned slow to pole back up. We should hit home by

Wednesday. By Thursday there'll be some Plank blood flowing in those hills."

The Partridge boys got into a gory discussion of who was going to do what to whom, and Shelter half-listened. He had no intention of becoming involved in their feud. He wanted Benton Gray.

They said Gray was in Nashville now, but would be returning soon. That fit Shelter's plan. The confrontation with a state senator in the capital was a bad idea. Better to meet him in the hills away from city eyes, officers of the law, newsmen.

They all agreed that they should leave as soon as possible. Shelter was given the responsibility of buying their horses. His own horse was lost somewhere in Mexico. They had come back across the Rio Grande, he and Elizabeth, riding a patient, hulking elephant named Nancy.

He found the horse market tough in New Orleans. The prices were high, the animals were enough to give a cowhand a cold sweat. Finally he bought five from a black man who had no papers on any of them but who had some fair stock and a decent price. He took Shell's gold furtively and slunk back into the jumbled, shadowed city to drink a part of it away.

Three of the horses were bays, branded hip and shoulder. One had a yellow menacing eye. Shell had selected a stocky gray for a pack animal, and a rangy buckskin with the Taxes KK brand smudged into a clumsy 88.

37

But they would be far from Texas and he had made the horse trader scratch out a bill of sale.

There was no patience in the Partridge boys nor in Duncan Corbett. They trailed out at sundown, knowing they could make no more than five miles before camp. But they had a killing anger in them and they were impatient for blood.

They camped deep in a bayou, watching the flaming sunset's last moments behind the black silhouettes of the swamp cypress. Spanish moss hung from the trees in damp boas, the light breeze twisted through the bayou and toyed with the fire.

Shelter sat apart from the others, sipping the scalding black coffee. They sat near to the fire, speaking in low slurred tones, their hill dialect becoming deeper, slashed by illusions, letting Shelter know that they regarded him as an outsider.

He spread a cloth and cleaned his pistol by the wavering firelight. Then, bothered only a little by the darting, humming mosquitoes, he tilted his hat across his eyes and slept.

At dawning they were on the move, splashing across the cypress lined Pearl River and into Mississippi where the land was still scorched, the houses still lying in ash heaps. A dozen black men picked at the mournful earth, not lifting their eyes as the Tennesseans rode by.

The Partridges were silent, gloomy. Their dark faces were stubbled, lined. "The boys don't say much," Shell commented.

"Ah, hell, you know how it is," Dunc answered, "they's hill folks. It'll take a time for them to get used to you, family or not."

"I had the feeling it was something else," Shell said.

Duncan glanced up sharply, his eyes hesitant in the shade cast by his torn flop hat. He started to lie, then admitted, "Yes, I guess there is somethin' else on the boys' minds."

"And it doesn't have anything to do with Dance Plank, does it?"

Duncan grinned. "I thought you might have caught that little lie." The kid was silent for a time, watching the backs of the Partridge boys who rode well ahead of them. There was a huge square patch in the middle of Bob's shirt.

He told Shell, "It's the old story been going around, Shelter. It's been cropping up since maybe ten years back. At the end of the war."

"What story?" Shelter wanted to know.

"Hell, you know."

"No I don't, Duncan," Shelter said in exasperation. "Why don't you tell me. Tell me the story and what it's got to do with the way the Partridge boys are acting."

"Sure." He sighed and glanced again at the Partridges. "You know, Shell, folks up around Pikeville and Whynot, we're poor as Preacher Possum. Times are hard, always have been, but since the war they's real bad. No grain, no stock, and cash money! — you'd have to shake the whole town of Whynot to find a copper penny."

"And so?"

"And so," Duncan said, nodding, "folks are hungry and resentful. Resentful of the Yankees, them grubbing carpetbaggers, Union laws, and rich folks."

"I don't think you could fit me into any of those categories, Dunc," Shell said.

"No?" Duncan glanced sideways at Shelter, then between his horse's ears at the Partridges once more. "Some say you're a rich man, Shelter."

"Me? I wouldn't have any objections," Shelter said with a smile, "but it's not so. What gives people that idea?"

"The story, Shelter. The story. You see it's told around that there was gold buried up near to Lookout. Left by Bragg, some folks say. Some say that during the war you ... requisitioned it from the Confederacy and rode off rich and grinning."

Shell was silent, grim-lipped. There was only one way that story could have gotten started. It was too close to the truth, in all but the essential element. It had to have come from Benton Gray's mind, a little protection maybe against the day Shell decided to come home? The thief, traitor, rich old Shelter Morgan? Was that the way it was supposed to work?

He glanced at Duncan, saying, "That's only

a story, Dunc. It's not true. Don't make the mistake of believing it yourself."

"Hell, Shelter," he exclaimed, "I never believed that—you're a Morgan. I mind your Daddy giving Widow Gaines a second cow after the one he sold her went dry through her own doin'. No, I never believed that trash." He said it, but there was doubt lingering in his eyes.

Shelter rode silently for a time. If the Partridge boys, his kin however distant, believed that, how did the rest of the valley feel? This was something he hadn't counted on.

He would be viewed with mistrust and maybe anger. Benton Gray was not only a state senator, but a friend to the hill poor, or so Duncan had told him. And Shelter Morgan? He was that sneak thief, that traitor, that flatland gunfighter.

He would have to ride softly, he decided. There were pillars of mistrust waiting to be toppled by any quick movement. When he looked again at Duncan Corbett, he saw the kid staring at him with measuring, undecided eyes.

They didn't like the feel of him, that flatland feel. How would they like it when he proved he had no intention of shooting Planks? When he went after Benton Gray?

It was something to be considered. These boys had no compunctions about shooting Planks from ambush or sniping at Union agents.

He doubted they would have few regrets about killing a Morgan if it came down to it.

It would do no good to protest innocence, to claim he knew nothing about a gold treasure. It would change nothing. The only way to stop these mountain boys was with a bullet.

3.

They found the Natchez Trace and rode northward, the air humid, stifling, the sun hot on their backs. It was three days north toward Tennessee and then two days eastward toward the great bulk of the Smoky Mountains.

They could see Lookout from twenty miles out, a great rounded brow of stone peering through the blue haze, and it gave Shelter a jolt. All of his boyhood memories were locked into these rambling broken hills, and some of his most vivid adult memories. That impossible, reckless recovery of the cache of gold under Union eyes. The moment of triumph, the exhilaration of the homeward march. Then the savage guns, the bitter long aftertaste of betrayal.

Duncan Corbett sat beside Shelter on the high ridge. The wind was in their hair and in the horses' manes. The long valleys below were flooded with maple and oak. Gold and autumn red. The falls up along little Damnation Creek were visible as a sliver of silvery glass against the stone bulwark of Old Man's Knoll.

"Feel good to be home?" Duncan asked.

"It feels strange, Dunc. Strange."

His mind roamed the paths of memory. There were bass in Damnation Creek, up near the big oaks. The water swirled in a pothole and there, in the morning shade, a man could take big mouth bass like plucking apples.

Nearer to Lookout, possibly along that ridge of Salt Back, Shelter had gotten himself cornered by a bear. A big, mean she-bear with one leg chewed off by a trap. A wild and canny thing, she bore down on Shell, and him all of ten years old with a smooth bore musket which might have been left behind by Pilgrims. He had one try, and he had touched off as she bellowed and pawed at him.

Then the bear had lurched and come down atop of him, smashing the breath from him.

44

He lay there, sure he was dead, sure he was going to feel those bear jaws clamp onto his skull. But she did not move, and Shelter panted and wriggled his way clear. When they turned that bear over they found the hair singed away around a musket ball hole.

There had been Sunday Socials at the church, a one-room school which was open only when they could find someone to act as teacher, long days of hoeing corn and firebright evenings when Pa would talk in his low, gravelly voice and Ma would do her needlework.

He couldn't see the old cabin from where they now sat, maybe it wasn't there. It was of stone and unbarked logs. A hundred years old when Shelter had been born. He didn't have the heart to ask Duncan about the old place, about the two graves beside the cabin. The one he and Pa had dug on a summer's eve, late. The other a lanky, lone boy had dug on his own, that year before the war.

"Let's get on down off this ridge," Shelter said, "it looks like it's a fixin' to blow."

Duncan glanced doubtfully toward the north where a jumble of clouds mushroomed skyward beyond Cumberland Mountain. It didn't look much like rain to him.

They wound through the pine and maple woods along Cherokee Trace in the late hours, the sun blinking through the clouds, the deep dark ranks of silent pines along the ridge.

The trail was a dark corridor through the head-high brush of blackthorn and scrub oak.

45

Corbett bobbed ahead of Shelter, behind him the Partridge brothers.

Abruptly there was a crimson rose blossoming beside the path. A fiery, eye-stunning rose and Sheltered wondered at it until a fraction of a second later the roar of the gun caught up with the muzzle flash.

Shelter's horse went nearly to his haunches and he saw Corbett's bay buckle at the knees. Bob Partridge jumped his horse into a thicket of blackthorn and a second shot rang from his gun.

Shelter dropped from his horse and plunged into the brush, his Colt automatically in his hand. He held the hammer back as he shouldered three paces into the brush and paused in the deepening, sunset cast shadows and listened, his heart hammering in his throat.

There were no more shots. He heard no one moving in the tangle of the thicket, but that did not surprise him. These were hill folks, woodsmen who survived by stealth.

His shirt clung to his chest. Perspiration wired down his throat. An owl called off on the high ridge. The pines along Salt Back Ridge were backlighted by deep orange light.

He heard a tiny sound. The gasp of a leaf being pressed underfoot and Shelter crouched lower. He saw the shadow, knew by the clothing it was not one of his people, and he sprang.

He roared out of the brush like a pampas bull and a rifle muzzle came up to meet him. Shell slapped the barrel aside and it exploded

46

over his shoulder, ringing like cathedral bells in his ears.

The gunman turned and ran and Shell sprinted after him. He wove through the brushy tangle, tripped on a hook of tree root and skidded down the leaf littered bank of a small creek.

Silent. Nothing but the water gurgling over stone. He crouched, panting. Then he picked his man out. He was scrambling up the far bank, a long haired, heavy hipped man and Shelter leaped up, splashing across the creek.

He lunged at the gunman, caught the heel of a boot and felt the boot wriggle free as the ambusher fell hard on his face. He was up in a hurry, but not quickly enough. Shelter was all over him.

He grabbed his hair and yanked, hooking his arm around the ambusher's neck. Rolling his prisoner over he got a surprise.

"A woman."

"Damn you to flamin' hell! Hell, yes I'm a woman. A Plank gal can shoot as good as any man!" She spat into his face and Shelter cuffed her, hard.

"Damn you," she sputtered again.

"Mind your manners and I'll treat you like a woman. Bark at me, spit on me and I'll treat you like I would a man—you got that?"

She nodded, her eyes wide. She relaxed some now under his grip and he surveyed her. She wore jeans and a man's plaid shirt, worn through at the elbows. There were a few buttons popped free and Shelter caught the rise and fall of smooth, full breasts beneath the shirt.

"Go ahead, do what you're going to," she said, going completely limp.

She was a pretty thing. Dark hair, cropped off at the shoulders, a full mouth, the under-lip protruding in a constant pout, and by the sundown light her eyes looked to be nearly purple behind thick, long lashes.

"I'm not going to do anything to you," he said, rolling away. Shelter stood, hovering over her in the darkness. She drew up her knees and touched her face gingerly.

"You're pretty rough," she complained. "Say, who are you? You're no Corbett."

"I'm a Morgan," Shelter answered.

"Ain't no Morgans left around here. Which one?"

"Shelter."

"Oh!" She looked him over again. "*That* one."

"And you are . . . ?"

"Violet Plank," she said coming to her feet. She glanced at Shelter's holstered Colt and then at his lean, dark face. "Shelter Morgan. They tell tales about you. Come back to kill my kin, did you?"

"I didn't come back to kill anybody, Violet. And I hope I don't have to. Especially no one as lovely as you."

"You can't flatter me!" she exploded. She cocked her head and stood, hands on hips, a challenging pout on those full lips.

"A woman like you needs the flattering, Violet. And," he added, "I wouldn't doubt you could do with a spanking now and again."

She opened her eyes wide, levelled a finger and then laughed. "You're right," she admitted. "You're not so bad, Shelter. Despite being agin' us."

"I'm not against you, Violet Plank. You or anyone else. Except for those folks who like to pot shoot at me. Like you were doing back there." He told her, "You get on out of here now before Dunc Corbett and the Partridge boys come hunting me. I've a notion they *would* shoot you."

"They'd try!" she snapped. That spark died quickly. She said soberly, "You're right. I'll be a-gettin'. Stay off the skyline, Shelter, and keep your powder dry."

She started past him and he reached out, taking hold of her shoulder, finding it remarkably strong. "The other way, Violet."

"Home's that way," she complained.

"I know it. And I know your gun's that way. Take my advice and try leaving guns alone for a while."

"I cain't get pot meat without my rifle," Violet objected.

"Try fishin'. Now get!" Shelter said. He smacked her hard on the rump and she turned an angry face to him. Then that anger dissolved into a smile and she walked into the trees, flitting through them as quietly as a shadow.

Shelter turned and slid down the steep bank,

49

splashing across the creek. It was nearly dark now, only a violet haze hanging between the mountain peaks, a last feeble gray light illuminating the path.

He found Violet's rifle and after a moment's thought propped it up in the crook of an oak. "I'm leaving it," he said quietly. There was no answer, but he knew she was out there. "Just mind how you use it."

He walked back to the trace, and saw the horses gathered, saw Duncan Corbett and the Partridge boys circled around a prostrate form.

Their heads turned around as he walked to them, and their rifles swung halfway toward him. "It's me, boys."

"Get the other one?" Dunc asked.

"Got clean away. What've you got?"

"Got us a Plank," Bob Partridge hooted. "Ready to skin and clean."

Shelter peered at the form on the ground. It was a kid, no more than fourteen, his eyes wide with hatred or fear or both. "Hell, he's not legal size. Better throw him back."

"His gun sure damn was legal size," Tom Partridge snarled. "What I am going to do is trim him down." His knife glinted in the starlight as he crouched over the kid. "I'm gonna start with this little pinky," Tom said, lifting the boy's hand. "Then maybe an ear, I haven't decided." His smile was sadistic, his voice throbbed with savage delight.

"Leave him be, Tom," Shelter said.

Partridge looked around as if he couldn't

believe his ears. "You tellin' *me* what do do, Morgan?"

"That's right. You back off with that blade. The kid was wrong, but I don't hold with what you have in mind."

"He killed a good horse tryin' to kill me!" Tom exploded. He turned back toward the kid, knife in hand.

"Let him up, Tom."

Shelter's voice was utterly flat, utterly cold. Tom Partridge squinted at Shelter as if he had not really seen him before.

"You're siding with them?"

"I'm not siding with them, Tom. Damnit, I just won't stand by and see a kid mutilated. Put that damned knife up before I take it away the hard way."

"You couldn't, big man."

"Don't bank on that." Shelter's hand rested on his holstered Colt, rested on it in a way which made the unspoken threat obvious. "Where's his gun?" Shelter asked.

Duncan Corbett handed it over, his eyes vastly disappointed. It was a beautiful piece, a Kentucky rifle with a bird's eye maple stock, a brass butt plate and some fancy scroll work on the barrel.

Shelter turned sharply, and with one hand smashed the rifle against a tree trunk, splintering the beautiful stock. The works he heaved deep into the underbrush.

"He won't be shooting at anybody else. Let him up."

51

Grumbling, Partridge stepped back and the kid rose shakily. "Damn you to hell, big man," the kid said. "I'd rather have lost my fingers and ears than lose that rifle!"

He stood, trembling before Shelter for a moment. Then starlight caught a crystal tear trickling down his ruddy cheek. The kid wiped it angrily away and stalked off into the night shadows.

The Partridge boys stood glaring at Shelter, Duncan shook his head as if that was the sorriest thing he had ever seen.

Shelter stepped into the saddle and Dunc, rigging the pack horse for riding whispered to Shell, "Maybe you ought to just swing that buckskin back toward New Orleans, Morgan. Seems I made a mistake. You've no business here."

"I'll guess I'll ride along with you," Shelter said. There was no answer. The moon, a silver splinter above the pines, drifted into the night sky.

It was a silent ride into the hills toward Whynot. Shelter knew he was being shunned now, and he wondered at the wisdom of riding with these boys in the first place. Yet the way it had turned out, a lone Shelter Morgan arriving in the hills would have been interpreted as badly. They could only have figured he had left some of his "treasure" behind and was coming to retrieve it.

Now, he knew with a certainty, he had enemies on both sides of this feud, and no friends remaining in these hills.

Whynot was a scattering of buildings—a
mill, a stable, a church-school combination
and a crossroads general store surrounded by
cabins which were secreted in the deep valleys
above the town.

It was said that Corbett and Morgan families
had founded the settlement, coming across
the smokies back in 1720. A weary woman
had pleaded with the men to stop somewhere,
anywhere, and Titus Morgan's reply had been
simply "Whynot?" thus providing a name for
the community. Later some unrecorded trouble
had led the Morgans back farther into the hills
to what was commonly called Pikeville but
which originally, as the old records showed,
had been Morgan Corners.

The town was silent, dark in the cradle of
the hills. They circled it and climbed the high
ridge trail toward the Partridge homestead,
a tilting shambles made up of a weather-grayed,
sagging cabin and three outbuildings, one of
which had fallen to the whims of gravity.

There was a lantern in the window. A coon
hound bayed in excitement and another joined
the discordant welcome.

Shelter knew that they would have already
been seen. There would be men posted in
the woods with the feud flaring.

Slowly they rode into the hard-packed yard,
tying up by the moonlight. Bob and Tom
Partridge went right on into the lighted cabin.

Shelter heard sounds of muffled welcome. Duncan Corbett unpacked the horses and threw the supplies they had not used on the trail into a gunny sack which he flipped over his shoulder.

"It's too late now, Shell. See if you can sweettalk the old man. Maybe he'll let it ride." Duncan's voice was unconvincing. Shelter slapped the trail dust from his pants and shirt and he stepped up onto the swayed stoop, following Dunc into the warm, smoky cabin.

There were ten people in the small room. The fire crackled in the stone fireplace. The old man sat in a wire-strapped rocker near the hearth, his long beard smoothed over his yellowed shirt, smoking a cob pipe.

This was the bull of the clan, old Jethro Partridge. A patriarch, a feudal lord in these hills. He had stern brown eyes around which dark circles ran. Beside him, against the wall, was his rifle. It was never out of reach, they said.

He lifted hard eyes to Shelter and he squinted through the wreath of smoke from his pipe.

Bob and Tom had already spoken to their pa, that was obvious by the way they watched expectantly. A nervous rail of a woman fussed over the stove which was sheet iron laid over rocks. Two stout hill men Shelter took for Corbetts stood flanking the old man.

"Shelter Morgan." The old man spoke without moving his lips any more than necessary. He looked Shell up and down and then turned his head and spat into the fireplace. "I ken ye. Ye've got yer daddy's features. Though yer stretched out a few more inches. And I hear ye've got yer daddy's ways."

"I don't kill pups, Mister Partridge, if that's what you mean."

"Pups!" he exlcaimed. He coughed with excitement. "Planks ain't pups, they's wolf whelps."

"Maybe. It's no different to me. I won't see a man mutilated." Shelter stepped nearer. "Did they tell you he was only fourteen, fifteen?"

"He had a gun!" Jethro Partridge hissed. "How old was Forrest Corbett when he was ambushed, Duncan?"

"Fourteen," Dunc said. He was leaning, arms folded, against the wall.

"Fourteen, Morgan. You fought that damned war. How many boys did ye see fourteen, fifteen who was a-firin' at ye?"

"Too many," Shelter said.

"I could kill ye fer what happened, Morgan," Jethro Partridge said. "Planks is our sworn enemy. You give 'em comfort. I got a daughter," Jethro nodded at a pretty quite pregnant girl who turned shy eyes away from Shelter and from Jethro's accusing, bony finger. "A Plank got her with whelp. A Plank!"

"The boy's dead, I understand. That ought to end it."

"End it? They ain't an end, boy, this side of the grave. I'll see ever' Plank buried." His eyes sparked with blood-excitement. Now he calmed, eyeing Shelter speculatively.

The old man hunched forward, speaking in a lower voice. "I'll let ye live, Morgan. For the sake of your daddy who done me a turn or two. I mind that you've been away from the hills. Your brain has gone flatland. I let yet live fer them reasons. Next time I cain't promise, Shelter Morgan. Next time mebbe I'll take you fer a Plank."

Bob and Tom Partridge seemed disappointed. Duncan's expression was unreadable. The bustling dried-up little woman served dinner at a long plank table and they sat to it, Shelter included.

The old man bowed his head and closed his eyes, muttering a rapid grace before they grabbed for the chicken and dumplings, talking all at once. Shell heard the door open behind him, saw the old man's eyes go hard. He nodded to Clemson Partridge. The fat man got up and strode past Shell whose head turned to follow him.

Two young women stood just inside the doorway. They were Clemson's Partridge's twin daughters, both blonde, ripe with the new bloom of maturity, pink cheeked, each with one front tooth slightly crooked, though that hardly marred the ripe beauty of the girls.

"Grace has been said," Clemson Partridge said menacingly.

"We was gathering blackberries, Pa, and . . . "

56

"No excuse. You have shamed me. Grace is done and you want to eat. Get your fannies outside, gals. To the woodhsed."

"No, Pa," one of them squealed, but Clemson pushed them on out. There was a flurry of shrill feminine protests and then the door was shut. Shell ate in silence, dipping his cornbread into the gravy. Jethro Partridge started in talking of local politics and his commentary finally swung around to Benton Gray.

Shelter asked no questions, tried to look disinterested, but he listened, trying to read the old man's attitude, which wasn't difficult.

"So Sheriff Dantley he tells Constable Rains to run Lavelle in, sayin' he done killed a man and he by-damned will be tried and hanged. And Rains, he's damned about ready to knuckle under to the Yankee Sheriff, but the matter is remarked to Senator Gray. He says, "Damnit, Sheriff, them hill folks have handled justice their own way for a hundred and fifty years. There's no point in tryin' to straighten this out. You'll likely nail the wrong party, disrupt the balance of power in Whynot.'" Jethro chuckled dryly.

"Disrupt the balance of power. I like that. That Benton Gray knows the hill folks won't stand for no scalawag law. It'd take an army to come in here and get Lavelle."

"He your grandson?" Shelter asked.

Jethro's eyes shifted to Shelter, the smile fading. "That's right. He's half again the size of you, Morgan, and twice the man. Flatland law tried to get him, but they wasn't quick enough or good enough."

"Benton Gray saved him?"

"Save him, hell. Lavelle don't need nobody's savin'. The senator just saw the right of it and called the scalawag dogs off."

"What did he do?" Shelter asked.

"Lavelle? He didn't *do* anything, Morgan. Flatland law claims he killed a young girl—sixteen years old. Claim he got mad when she wouldn't spread for him—sorry Ma. Hell, Lavelle could get any be-damned woman he takes a liking to. Couldn't of happened that way and Benton Gray knows it."

Jethro Partridge leaned back proudly puffing his chest. "Lavelle will be comin' home soon. Have ye a look, Morgan. Because there's a man for ye."

The door opened again and the twins came in, their eyes red. They rubbed their rumps through the thin calico of their faded dresses.

Sniffling they sat opposite Shelter, quietly accepting their supper. Carrie and Cassie Partridge were their names. Two full-bodied, healthy young women. Their eyes were downcast as they ate, but from time to time Shell caught one of them glancing at him with earthy interest.

The old woman had started washing the dishes, silent and weathered as old wood. Jethro rose and went out onto the stoop and the men followed him. They sat smoking their pipes, talking in low voices.

Shelter finished his plate and walked to the kitchen where the old woman washed the dishes in a battered galvanized tub.

"Want me to help you, Mrs. Partridge?" Shelter asked.

She turned to him, her dark eyes staring out of a sunken face and she spoke with a voice which creaked, which seemed dusty as if it was seldom used and never above a whisper.

"Ain't fittin'," was all she said.

Shelter walked back into the big room, and the girls broke into giggles as they saw him.

"Tall, ain't ye?" one of them asked.

"Not so tall as Lavelle, I've been told."

"Him!" one of the twins answered with a disgust which made it apparent they didn't share Jethro Partridge's high opinion of the man.

"He's tall and big," the other girl said. "But small in the brain. And he's got a tiny black heart."

"He's kissin' kin, but I'd never kiss him. Be afraid my lips would turn black and drop off." She stood, circling Shelter, her musky fragrance filling his nostrils.

"You're kissin' cousin too, Shelter Morgan," the girl said. Her sister giggled. "I'm Cassie. If you ever feel like a little kissin', you let me know."

"I don't think your Pa would favor that, nor would Jethro."

"Them! They's old and dry." She spoke bravely, but Shelter noticed that her eyes flickered hastily toward the closed door. "All they want of life is the killin' and the drinkin'."

"You want more, Cassie?"

"A lot more." She leaned nearer. "Ask me some time and I'll tell you everything I want, Cousin."

She rested a hand on Shell's shoulder and he gently removed it. Polly Partridge sat sewing in the corner, her round, pregnant figure slumped miserably. The old woman was not looking, but her ears had to be listening. This was no time, no place for stirring things up more than they already were.

"We'll talk another time," Shelter said.

"You can bet on that, Shelter Morgan," Cassie said in a husky voice. Then she and her twin were engulfed by laughter again. Shell picked up his hat and blanket roll, glancing again at the twins, at Polly who sat making clothes for a baby. He thought of the baby's father, dead and buried now because of the feud, and he wondered what went on in Polly's mind when she thought of it.

Maybe she didn't think of it. Maybe she figured she had no right to. It was the code of the hills. They were right in killing Aaron Plank; she was wrong in what she did. The law seemed to support her family. Benton Gray's law.

Maybe nothing at all was going on in that mind besides thinking about the next stitch and the next. Maybe they had killed Polly Partridge that day they had shot up Aaron

Plank. Maybe Polly's life would be just like it was now for the rest of her days. One stitch after the next until she was as dried up, dusty and used as the old woman.

As Shelter stepped out onto the stoop all eyes turned to him.

"Going somewhere?" Jethro asked. He had a jug of corn liquor.

"Thought I'd spread my roll in the timber. I'm used to sleeping outside."

"Are ye?" the old man asked wryly. "I understood ye flatlanders slept in ho-tels. Dunc say he found ye there." He smiled sourly, and Shelter knew that was not all he had told the old clan chief.

"I'll see you men in the morning," Shelter said.

"With a little luck," Bob Partridge said, spitting.

"I won't be around long," Shelter told them. He leaned briefly against the upright, watching the star glazed mountains. "I know when I'm not wanted."

"Don't need no flatland sissies," Tom Partridge said. Shelter shot him a hard glance, but said nothing.

"Where be ye going, Morgan?" the old man asked.

"Up to the old place, if it's still there."

"It be there. Nothin' left though."

"A few memories. I'll see to Ma and Pa's graves."

"That's fittin'," the old man said, nodding as he sucked on his pipe stem. "Ye go on and do that, Morgan. But be ye keepin' yer head low, hear? There's Planks a-roamin', and they'll be a-shootin'."

"Planks or Partridges?" Shelter asked.

"Us!" The old man acted offended. "We be kin, Shelter Morgan."

He said it in earnest, it seemed, but there was a cackle of laughter from the porch as Shelter nodded and walked off into the dark, cold woods.

Cassie Partridge had sidled out onto the porch, her hands clasped behind her back and she started down into the yard. Her father reached out and grabbed her calf.

"Where be ye goin', Cassie?" Clemson Partridge demanded.

She lifted her eyes to the woods and she said, "I come to find I lost my tortoise-shell comb, Pa. Thought I should go lookin'."

"I ken what you're goin' lookin' fer, Cassie," he replied sharply. "Get your tail back in the cabin."

"Pa?" she pleaded.

"Get! Before I take the switch up again."

She nodded dismally and shuffled back into the house, her bare feet whispering over the gray, weathered planks.

"Sooner he's done with the better," Clemson Partridge said, looking toward the woods himself.

"Don't be rushin' it, Clem," Jethro said. The

old man's eyes sparkled slyly in the starlight. "I ain't so sure I want that Morgan boy run off or done under jest yet. The boy's come back for somethin'. Ain't fer the fightin'. What then, Clem? What fer did Shelter Morgan come back? They's an answer, and I mind we find it before the killin' of him comes due." He relit his pipe and nodded, "And that time will come for the boy. He ought never have crossed his family. A traitor to the clan, why he's worth nothin' alive. No," he shook his bearded chin, "I reckon we all know what will have to be done in the end."

He looked toward the pine woods and then to the starry skies. Then, with satisfaction Jethro Partridge stood, scratched his belly and stuffed his pipe into his pocket.

"Night boys. There's things to be done to-morrow, and I'm gettin' to where I need my rest."

4.

Shell made his bed deep in the woods, high up on a mossy ledge. He thought no one could come upon him without being heard, and he was not worried about sleeping too soundly despite the trail weariness.

There was too much going on in his head, too much to think about, and the thoughts flitted about inside his skull, nagging at him.

He had started wrong. He had made an enemy of the Partridges. By birth he was an enemy of the Planks, the way the hill folks saw it.

So here he was between both sides, a target for any man who happened to be carrying a rifle. (Or any woman, he thought, recalling Violet Plank.)

Not only that, but they all figured he had some gold hidden up on Lookout. Consequently they figured him for a thief and a traitor to the South—enough cause in these hills for a man to be shot down.

Chiefly Shell thought of Benton Gray. He peered through the dark boughs of the deep pines, watching the blue diamonds of the stars in the high sky, watching the tips of the trees sway in the slight breeze. He propped his head up and rested his clasped hands behind his neck.

Gray. A killer turned eminently respectable. A state senator. A *beloved* state senator. So what did Gray have to do with the somewhat sullied Lavelle Partridge? Why did the senator go out of his way to see that the big, vicious grandson of Jethro Partridge was not molested by the law? For that matter, with all the fine homes in Nashville and Natchez, the graces of Knoxville, the social advantages of Chattanooga, why did Benton Bray choose to stay in this political and intellectual backwater? To flatter his constituents? If so, he was breaking new political ground.

There was something there, like a tight knot which Shelter could not get a hold on. It kept slipping through his mental fingers. Finally he gave it up, watching a sheer blanket of cloud drift before the moon and scattered stars.

He thought again of that high cabin, his home, if home he had. And briefly, before his eyes closed, Shelter thought of Elizabeth, pictured her arriving in Washington on a train. He wondered what she thought of this night.

His head came up sharply.

Something had moved off in the pines. His hand went to the Colt which rested beside his leg beneath his blue blanket.

He peered into the inky shadows, seeing nothing. He heard only the whisper of the wind in the trees. And then he did see it.

Or her. He thought it was a woman, and he thought first of Cassie. He cursed, silently, damning the knuckle-headed brains of the girl. But it was not Cassie.

He saw her skittle through the trees, a narrow, hunched figure with dark hair, the wind pressing her heavy skirt to her legs. Shelter started to rise, then settled back, his heart thumping, seeing she was gone.

No, it was not Cassie, nor Violet Plank. His heart was racing like a child's frightened heart because that was where he knew her from — if it was her. From childhood.

He had seen her standing over his mother's fog-shrouded grave, waving her arms in eerie circles, chanting weirdly and he had cried out.

She had turned toward his lantern at the sound, a seamed, craggy woman with an outlandish nose and fearful dark eyes. She was bent up, crooked and horrible. She had cackled shrilly as Shelter ran, dropping his lantern, toward the house.

When he had reached it, he had slammed the door behind him, and stood, panting, holding the door with all of his might.

That was the night he had first seen her, although he saw her many times after, flitting through the woods gathering toadstools and moss, centipedes and bats.

The Witch Woman, they called her. Or the Witch of the Mountain. There were terrible stories about her—she baked pies with the meat from little boys and girls. She could fly like a bat, screech like an owl and slither like a snake.

The children all hurried home after dark.

It seemed she must have been a hundred years old then, although kids often overestimate age. But she was older than anyone they had heard of, older than old Ben Yount who had fought in the Revolution, or so he said.

She was still alive then, still haunting the woods. But why here, Shelter wondered, why now? He lay back and closed his eyes once more. He slept then, more deeply than he would have believed possible, it seemed, for when he opened his eyes it was already gray in the eastern sky with false dawn's light.

There was a heavy dew on the grass, clinging to the trees as Shelter rolled out, tying his bed and ground sheet up. He walked through the pine woods, coming to the creek he had forded the evening before.

He looked around seeing nothing but the hesitant orange of sunrise beyond Lookout Mountain, a fleet-footed family of quail, and so he stripped, stacking his clothes on a rock beside the river.

The water was icy enough to turn his flesh blue. His bones felt brittle under his skin from the cold, and his teeth chattered. But he had been on the trail for days, his last bath had been miles back. He had spent too many army days, too many trail days dusty and grimy not to appreciate a wash-up anytime he got the chance, cold or not.

Shelter scrubbed his chest, squatted down to immerse himself briefly, then rising, he swept back his dark hair and stepped from the water.

Giggling.

He heard the giggling and turned toward the stand of oaks, naked and cold in the morning light. He could not see the twins there, but he knew there were only two girls in the county who giggled like that—a rising, chesty giggle which Shelter imagined could get annoying real quick.

"Show's over," he said. He picked up his pants and stamped into his boots. Pulling on his shirt, he stood watching the sun top Lookout. A golden filament outlined the bald mountain crest. Then it flushed crimson and withdrew from the shadows of night, standing stark and unyielding.

Lookout had been scarred during the war. Bragg had used it, then withdrawn to Missionary Ridge. Then Hooker had reenforced General Thomas' Union forces and the bloody Battle Above the Clouds had been fought, with Hooker's men dislodging Longstreet and Bragg.

Lookout had been scarred by cannonfire, honeycombed with tunnels and gun emplacements, but in the end the mountain prevailed and the men, broken and bloodied, had been shattered while Lookout Mountain endured, stoic, immutable.

Shelter hefted his roll and walked across the bed of pine needles through the early morning shadows. A crow called, circling against the crystal sky. Someone had arrived at the Partridge cabin.

Shell saw the big gray mule standing beside his buckskin horse, and he knew it meant trouble. He had gotten only halfway across the yard when the big man stepped out onto the stoop.

He was a hulking bear of a man with a tangled black beard and huge shoulders bursting at the seams of his torn white shirt worn under faded overalls. He had tiny dark eyes, those eyes which reflect at once a congenital stupidity and a vicious tendency.

He wanted a fight. Shelter could read that in his face as well. An arrogant savagery lurked there. Lavelle Partridge, due to his size and nature, had probably never lost a fight of any kind in his life. He had the neck of an ox, the wrists of a blacksmith. He came forward, watching Shelter from the porch, his wide black shadow smeared against the gray wood of the cabin.

Shelter stopped, tied his roll onto his saddle and cinched up. He ignored Lavelle Partridge, he wanted none of this. Lavelle wanted to push it, though; he read Shelter's actions as cowardice.

"You Cousin Morgan?" Lavelle demanded. Shell heard the porch creak as the big man stepped from it. Shell didn't bother responding.

"You gonna say hello, Cousin Morgan," Lavelle said. His voice was nearer now. There was taunt in his words, and Shelter knew it was inevitable.

"Hello, Lavelle," Shelter said, turning. Lavelle was nearly on top of him, the stink of his body strong. His beady eyes glared out of his puffy face.

"Thought you was deaf as well as dumb, Morgan," Lavelle said. Over his shoulder Shelter could see the clan gathered on the stoop. Cassie had turned her face away, burying it in Carrie's shoulder. Jethro Partridge's face was hard and sharp as a hatchet. It was clear what the old man expected — teach the flatlander a lesson.

"Don't push it, Lavelle," Shelter said in a voice so low that the big man was the only one who heard him.

"Don't push it!" Lavelle bellowed. "Push

70

what? Don't you like me, Morgan? I heerd
you didn't like Partridges. Only Planks, is that
it? Or is it just plain yellow guts?"

He leaned over Shelter, his breath rancid.
He stank of whisky and grime. Lavelle must
have gone six-six and from the bloated look
of him he was nearer to three hundred than
two.

Shelter turned away and Lavelle started to
grab at him. Shell felt the pawing hand on
his shoulder and without turning he cracked
back with his elbow, lifting it high. The elbow
point caught Lavelle in the chest and a whoosh
of air escaped. Lavelled staggered backward
a step, his face going crimson.

Shelter turned, slowly unbuckled his gunbelt and fastened it over the pommel of his
saddle.

Lavelle was rubbing his chest and he muttered, "That was pure unfriendly, cousin. You
have opened the ball now. I hate to do it, but
I'm going to have to break you up, Cousin
Morgan."

"We can stop right here, Lavelle. Forget
it and I'll ride out."

"No," he wagged his heavy head. "There's
no choosin' now. It's got to be done."

Shelter took a deep slow breath. He tossed
his hat over his gunbelt and watched as Lavelle

71

slowly circled, hands held low. The light was slanting through the oaks. The air was cool. Tiny puffs of dust rose from beneath Lavelle's clodhoppers.

The big man was surprisingly light on his feet. Shell had to duck away from a sudden left hook and he was caught by a following right hand from Lavelle. The punch caught him flush, with all of Lavelle's bulk behind it and the lights blinked on in Shelter's skull.

He thought it was all over right then. Through the cobwebs he could see a distorted Lavelle-face grinning at him, drooling with savagery. Shelter back-pedaled, side-stepped and ducked, shaking his head trying to clear the fog as Lavelle pursued him.

Through the haze he could see Jethro Partridge, Duncan, the twins all watching him. Lavelle's fist boomed in from out of the haze and caught Shelter again and he felt his legs go rubbery. He swam out of the murkiness and managed to throw up a left arm just in time to block a murderous right hand.

A left caught him on the shoulder where the nerves are webbed up over the joint and Shelter's arm went numb.

Now with his right partially dangling, Shelter bobbed away, sticking his left efficiently into Lavelle's face. He popped him with that straight jab. Popped him again, and again, watching as the blood trickled from Lavelle's wide nose, but it was hardly slowing the big man down.

He still wore that mocking smile and he hunched his shoulders as he came in at Shelter, winging rights and lefts. Shelter took a heavy body shot just above the liver, but answered with his best shot of the fight, a hard right hook which snapped Lavelle's head back.

The fog was starting to clear and Shelter's body was starting to respond, to warm to the task. Lavelle seemed a little slower. Maybe he had thrown his best shots already.

Just as Shelter thought that, he found himself rocked by a hammering right which slipped over his guard, glancing off his skull at the temple.

Lavelle hooked hard to Shelter's ribcage and Shell backed away, fighting for breath. But Partridge came in too confidently and Shell was able to place a nifty, damaging left just below Lavelle's jawline, slamming it against the hard meat of his neck.

Lavelle roared and came in, ducking low. Shelter threw an uppercut from the ground and Lavelle's head jolted back. He must have bitten his tongue, for instantaneous, profuse blood flowed from between Lavelle's yellow teeth.

Panting and pawing Partridge came in steadily, Shelter jabbing and staying outside. He feinted right and then came left, inside. He tromped down hard on Lavelle's instep, threw a flurry of blows to the heart and wind and stepped out, Lavelle limping after him, his face smeared with blood now.

"Get him, Lavelle," Jethro called. It was not encouragement, it was an order and Lavelle did his best to comply.

He aimed a savage kick at Shell's kneecap, trying to kick it off, to break the bone to a bag of marbles, but Shelter saw it coming and stepped back. Lavelle was off-balance as he kicked and Shelter grabbed his boot as it came up, swinging it through the arc, lifting Lavelle's leg higher until the brawler lost his balance and went down hard on his back.

The breath was slammed out of Lavelle Partridge and he went white behind that black beard. Heavily the big man got to his feet, his face smeared with mingled blood and yellow dust.

Some of the confidence seemed to have washed out of Lavelle's button eyes. He flinched when Shelter feinted with a left, but the big man wasn't going to quit. He plodded on in, encouraged by the cheers of the clan.

He whiffed a right at Shelter, but it was a slower punch than those he had thrown earlier and Shelter ducked, the big fist glancing off his shoulder. Shell continued to prod and sting, looking for the opening he wanted as they circled.

The sun was hot on his back now. His shirt was plastered to his body with perspiration. His shoulder was numb, his ribs sore, his lungs afire. Lavelle limped in and Shelter peppered him with lefts, the big man's head bouncing with each blow.

"Do him, Lavelle!" Jethro ordered and Lavelle nodded wearily, coming in on Shelter with determination. He lifted a left too slowly and Shelter countered with a sharp right which landed on Lavelle's ear. He tried it again with the same result. Panic began to build in Lavelle Partridge's dark little heart. He knew now that Shelter was growing quicker as his own arms grew heavy. And, Morgan's blows were being timed better now. They snapped against his face like whip cracks.

With a fury of rage and frustration Lavelle lunged forward, his arms like windmills. He threw all he had, lefts and rights. When he had no luck that way he hurled himself at Shelter, intending to take him to the ground to bite, gouge and stomp the man senseless.

Lavelle was quick, but not in that kind of move. He threw himself at Shelter but Shell stepped aside and Partridge landed flat on his face, his tremendous body quivering for a moment. He rose to hands and knees and Shelter, weary of it, planted his foot and kicked out, his boot toe catching Lavelle on the point of his furry chin.

Lavelle's head cracked backward and he rolled onto his side, pawing at the ground, trying to rise.

Lurching to his feet he swayed badly, but he lifted his fists, meaning to take it all the way. Shelter faked with his head and then it was there. The big opening he had been waiting for. Lavelle's eyes followed Shelter's head and the big man's left dropped low.

Shelter was ready. He brought the right up from his waist, with all the push of his legs and hips behind it. He axed Lavelle with the blow, dropping the big man in his tracks.

Lavelle's eyes rolled back and he dropped like a sack of potatoes to the earth. He twitched as if he would rise, but the motions were involuntary. He made an odd little whimpering sound deep in his bearded throat and then lay utterly still, completely silent. The dust sifted through the band of sunlight through the oaks and settled.

Shelter turned and walked to his horse. He saw Bob Partridge step forward, his rifle in hand. But Shelter was around in the blink of an eye, his Colt levelled.

"Stand steady, Bob. No need to die on this pretty morning."

Partridge froze. Jethro Partridge spat on the ground, then he waved a threatening finger. "This ain't over, Morgan. Not by a long shot."

Shelter nodded at Lavelle. "It is for him, Jethro."

Then with a bravado Shelter did not feel

he stepped into the saddle and rode out, his back to those rifles. He rode two miles at a walk, his head aching, his breathing still ragged. He found Wolf Creek and stepped down, letting the buckskin drink as he bathed his hands in the icy water.

Rinsing his face Shelter stood. He looked at the shredded shirt he was wearing, tore what was left of it off and took the new blood red shirt from his saddlebags.

A trickle of blood still leaked from his scalp into his eyes and he dabbed at it from time to time until it stopped. His hands were stiffening up fast. He flexed them, finding he had been lucky—no broken bones. A man's skull is solid, and it's no place to throw a bare-handed blow if you can help it. But it's instinct to do so, and Shelter had followed that instinct murderously.

By now Lavelle would be propped up, belting down some raw crackcorn, and they would be figuring what they wanted to do next.

Maybe they would do nothing. Shelter must be secondary to their main plan—the war on the Planks. With luck, he told himself hopefully, he would be finished with his business and out of the hills before Jethro Partridge decided to come after him again.

Lookout Mountain cast a broad, brash shadow across the deep valleys. Shelter let his horse pick its way along the seldom used, partly overgrown paths which hung out into space above swift, narrow rills and at other points dipped down into the river bottoms to follow the fern-rich gorges.

It was a jumbled, jagged land. In some of these deep valleys the sun shone for only an hour or so a day. Bare rock punctured the velvet green of the earth, and pine, maple, oak and birch clung tenaciously to the thin soil. Here and there violets flooded a bench or bottom. Rhododendron competed with marsh marigolds and the fern for growing space.

Higher up the birch stood among the pines, their slender white trunks like bleached bones against the shady backdrop of the cold blue-green pines. A cougar flitted behind the trees and was gone like a pale golden ghost. The white tail doe Shelter's intrusion had saved from the cougar turned tail and leaped into the underbrush.

It was a beautiful, but almighty sorrowful place. Shelter had begun to pass places he knew well, altered only slightly by memories' ways. Changeless—the black oak split in half by summer lightning, the polished gray rock of the swimming tank, cut by eons of gushing water.

All the same, vastly different. For though the land had not changed, the man had. The things he recalled had happened far away, to a different person. There was no delight in this homecoming, only a solemn appreciation.

The wind gusted up, blasting against man and horse as they crested the ridge. The pine there were flagged by the wind, the branches growing only on one side. These needled tentacles trembled violently in the wind. Shelter sat the ridge, looking back toward the Partridge cabin, invisible now behind the trees, toward Whynot where a thin tendril of smoke weaved its way skyward.

The valleys below were splotches of vivid gold, deep crimson, shades of purple behind the film of blue-gray haze. Ahead lay Pikeville and beyond that the homestead. Above it all Lookout Mountain loomed.

He wondered where exactly Benton Gray's house was. Duncan had placed it between Pikeville and Whynot just about midway, but Shelter had not been able to see the ranch — where supposedly Gray was breeding Tennessee Walkers. But then there were many ridges between here and there, and as Shell knew too well an army could be concealed in the hollows.

He found little Hatchet Creek, now dry, and followed it homeward. It struck him funny that he knew the approach to this valley better from the other side, from the Georgia line. Every inch of that high-ridge trail into and out of Tennessee was etched permanently in his mind, as permanently as the death of Keane, of Dinkum and Thornton. The location of the gold cache he could probably find again, but oddly he had little recollection of digging it up, save for the smell of the damp earth.

He was suddenly there. A quintet of hundred-year old pines swayed slightly in the wind.

The creek ran silver-bright across the meadow. The old stone well. The corncrib. And a tiny stone cabin, square and squat, the log roof bowed by winter's weight. Shelter let the buckskin make its way into the valley. Home.

The breeze brought the sweet scent of grass, the notched swayback ridge cut jagged patterns against the autumn sky. A pair of cottontails kicked out of the brush underfoot and zigzagged toward the timber.

Shell swung down in the overgrown yard, looking at the boarded up window. He had done that the day he left for the army. Pa had brought that single pane of glass all the way from Charleston as a Christmas surprise for his mother. She had laughed and hugged them both.

"Now," she said, "I'll have sun while I work, it'll be like having the jays and the gray squirrels right in the kitchen with me."

Pa had made some sort of joke about that, a joke which was lost to Shelter's memory. But he hadn't forgotten the joy of his mother, the almost surgical care with which his father had fitted the new window.

He left the gray to tug at the long grass which grew up to and through the porch. The graves stood beneath the old black oak.

He took off his hat and walked to them, reading his father's skilled inscription on the slab of maple which was his mother's headstone, then shifting his eyes to the cruder, somewhat matching marker he had made for Pa that night.

He remembered his mother's pale, patient face as she lay a-dyin', her hands folded over the quilt, her hair drifted out on the pillow. Closing his eyes he could also recall vividly the terrible night Pa had come in after a trip to Whynot for supplies. He had moved shakily and Shelter had made him sit.

"What is it, Pa?"

"Nothin', I reckon, Shell. Little pain in my back. It hit me in Butler's Store. Like a little kink that won't go away."

Later he had trouble with his breathing and took a drink of brandy—rare for Pa—to still the pain in his back and chest. By morning he was dead.

With both of them gone Shelter had tried to work the land, but it was no good. Then the war had come and Shelter had gone a-fightin'.

He felt suddenly cheated, standing there in the shade of the old black oak. Not by events, but by time which seemed to be unravelling too rapidly now. Far too rapidly.

He cleaned up around the graves and picked some violets for Ma. Pa would have scoffed at it, so he left his father's grave unadorned. With surprise Shelter realized that the sun had dropped behind the ridges. It was cooler and growing dark, a slow purple haze seeping into the bowl of the valley.

Shelter unsaddled the buckskin and picketed

it in the yard where the grass was high, lush. He rubbed the horse's back with a handful of long grass, watching evening fall.

What made him decide he did not know. He had planned on sleeping out, then suddenly he decided to sleep inside. The door opened on wooden hinges and Shelter stepped into the musty interior of the old cabin. Dropping his saddle in a corner he found a candle, covered with the dust of the years and lighted it.

It flared up weakly, illuminating the dusty, scrambled interior of the house. Someone, kids perhaps, had been inside. The chairs were tipped over, the cupboards open. A nest of pack rats, now absent, had lived in the fireplace for a time and an owl had been in there, messing up things in a way only an owl has the talent for.

Poking around Shelter found a lantern and in the bottom of an ancient gallon can, a dab of coal oil. He lit the lamp and placed it on the table, standing the chairs to the table.

The broom was in the corner, cobwebbed, some of the straws pulled free by the pack rats for their nest-making. With that he poked at the clogged chimney, dislodging pounds of soot and three long-unused swallows' nests.

The frame and headboard of the good solid bed his father had carved from oak was there, but the small animals had chewed away the leather strapping and dug into the ticking, so Shelter rolled out his bed on the floor.

What was he doing? Cleaning up the place,

a house where he would not stay? In a month it would look the same as it had when he opened the door.

He sat at the table, drinking some coffee in a blue ceramic cup he had found and boiled out. The lantern flickered low.

Maybe the key to it all was that somewhere, deep inside, he wanted to stay, to stop his hard-trailin', the killing, the bloodshed. Maybe there was a Shelter Morgan hidden away inside who wished for nothing more than a warm cabin, a few acres of good earth.

He shrugged those thoughts away, finishing with them as he finished his coffee. It was, he told himself, just a reaction to the dust and the litter which defaced the warm memories of the cabin. That and nothing more.

He rolled up in his bed, listening to the night sounds, staring long at the roof overhead, the embers in the fireplace.

The shots brought him out of his bed with a lunge.

5.

The shots echoed out of the woods, thudding into the pine of the cabin, whining madly off the stone chimney. Shelter was next to the door, pressed to the wall.

The shots came in a volley. Rifle fire spaced almost rhythmically as if it were the result of a man firing, levering in a cartridge, firing again. Repeating the pattern again with obviously no target in mind but the cabin itself.

There was the sound of shattering glass

and Shelter glanced toward the window, breathing a long, ornate curse. "Sorry, Ma," he said. Her window lay in shards against the floor of the cabin.

The rifle fire ceased and Shelter tensed. Maybe they would make their move now, figuring they had softened him up enough.

He pulled away from the door, upturned the table and got behind it, awaiting their rush. The hearth was still warm behind him. The seconds ticked but but no one came. It was silent as death, empty as the moon.

Shelter eased to the door and swung it open with his foot, ducking away, expecting a hail of gunfire.

Nothing.

He studied the woods across the meadow by the silver moonlight, seeing nothing. He slipped into the night, pressing close to the cabin. He held his Colt beside his ear and rounded the corner of the cabin, gun barrel first.

No one there, nor around back. He circled the cabin and then searched the outbuildings, the tumble-down tool shed, the barn.

It was dead silent. Only the stars answered his questioning gaze. They had pulled off. Maybe someone just wanting to intimidate him. Who? Jethro Partridge? Maybe, but it didn't seem to be the old man's style. Shelter had a hunch the clan chief would see that the job was done quickly, neatly.

Maybe the Planks. They could know, through Violet, that he was back. But wouldn't they have simply waited until he stepped out onto the porch in the morning and shot him where he stood?

Shelter frowned against the night. Maybe some drunk shooting at what he assumed to be an empty place—as it had been empty for so long. Then Shelter's eyes picked up his nervous buckskin across the meadow, and he knew that anyone in the woods would have seen the horse as well, and known the place was occupied.

He moved warily back to the cabin, went in and barred the door. There was no puzzling it out tonight, and he meant to sleep, although he would not sleep as well as he might have.

Morning was a stream of light through the broken window, the shattered shutters. Shelter watched the ray of light creep slowly across the floor of the cabin, yawning as he stayed burrowed in his blankets against the chill of morning.

When he was a kid he stayed lazily abed until Pa crossed the room and got the morning fire blazing. He would lay and watch Pa shave, watch Ma bustle about the kitchen, the strong rich smell of coffee filling the room and later the enticing scent of bacon frying.

There would be no bacon frying on this morning, and if there were to be a fire, Shelter knew he would have to start it himself. It wan't worth it, not for a man alone and so he rose in the chill and stamped into his boots, taking a tin of beef from his saddlebags. He opened it with his bowie and sat at the table, eating the cold, fatty meat.

Sunlight sparkled on the dew-fresh grass when he stepped out into the morning. Moving with caution, Shelter saddled his horse, remaining on the off-side from the woods.

Walking the buckskin across the meadow he entered the woods at a point opposite the front door of the cabin. He cast back and forth for a ways before he found the spot. The grass was pushed down and a handful of cartridge cases lay scattered on the grass.

Forty-four-forties, too common to be of any help. He twirled the casing and studied the area more closely. One man had done all the shooting, but there were two sets of footprints. The other man had stood holding the horses. An odd tactic for an assault force. Both men could have been firing.

All right then, they had only wanted to chase Shelter off. Why would that be? Benton Gray, the Partridges, Planks . . . all would have preferred to kill him.

He flipped the cartridge away and walked on, staying on the edge of the woods, following the tracks left by the two riders.

At the Pikeville Road they turned toward town and were lost in the mass of tracks and wagon ruts. All sorts of vehicles, heavy vehicles, had been using that road, and many horses. Too many.

Just where the hell was everyone going? The

road drifted out of Pikeville, cut Fainer's Valley, and Lone Pine—total population about twenty people. Then the road, only a trail after Lone Pine, wound up toward . . . Lookout Mountain.

Shelter's eyes lifted to the mammoth, cold stone of Lookout and he frowned. Unless he was reading everything wrong somehow, there was a hell of a lot of traffic up to the mountain. That made no sense at all. Maybe Lone Pine was suddenly booming. But there were no gold strikes and such as Shelter had seen in the western mountains, no boom towns like Leadville and Silver City. Lone Pine had only about a hundred acres level enough to do anything with, and that was all in hay and corn. Or had been.

Shelter had to keep reminding himself that he had been away a long time. A lot can change in ten years. All of this was far from his purpose—finding Benton Gray. But a man finds himself growing curious when he's shot at.

He thought of Gray as he rode toward Pikeville. Wealthy, popular, powerful. He had only one fear in his world, probably. The fear that Shelter Morgan would return, upsetting it all.

Against that possibility Benton Gray had carefully fabricated a lie of a life for Shelter. He had stolen Confederate gold, murdered his own men, ridden west wealthy and arrogant. So the story went, and it was believed, apparently.

He thought again of the sniping at the cabin

and wondered if Gray knew that Shelter was back. If not, he undoubtedly would soon. Maybe Jethro would see to it, personally.

That way he would be getting rid of Shelter who had gone against him, and there would be a favor done for Benton Gray, a favor the senator would remember. There might even be a cash reward in Jethro's hand by now.

Gray would know by now, Shelter had no doubt. Ride lightly, he reminded himself. The wolf's got teeth.

Pikeville was a collection of five shingle-sided buildings pushed together at the vortex of seven different ridges which fell together at this particular point. The geologic calamity which had shoved the ridges up and slammed them against each other had also broken open a deep spring. It was the main reason Pike-ville still existed, Shelter supposed.

He knew no one he saw on the streets. Four men, all strangers, knotted together on a corner, eyes lifting as Shell dragged the street on his buckskin.

He could think of only one man he knew who was not a Partridge, a Plank or a Cor-bett. Chase Miller, if he was still alive, would be at his work in the blacksmith's shop. He had been a friend of Pa's, and a friend of Grand-pa's. A wiry, white-haired man with hands like talons, clear gray eyes and a no-nonsense approach to life, Miller had always had time to listen to the youngsters.

Shelter had spend uncounted hours watching

Chase fire the forge, beat red, sparking metal into wheel rims, barrel strapping, horseshoes and handtools.

Out of habit Shelter walked the buckskin to the rear of the blacksmith's shed and entered by the back door. The smell of sulphur and slag filled his nostrils. It was hot inside, the furnace glowing a dull orange. Chase Miller was at the bellows, pumping enthusiastically, his eyes intent. His lips moved as he talked to himself, eyeing the fire, the tongs he held.

"Hello, Chase."

The old man's head came around. He glanced at Shelter, muttered, "Jest a minute," then turned back sharply, peering at Shell.

"Shelter Morgan?" he asked.

"It's me, Chase."

"Damn me for a Yankee!" He came forward, his shoulders slightly hunched, his hawk eyes sharp and clear. He wiped his hand on the leather apron he wore and thrust it out.

Shelter took the hand warmly. He was not surprised by the strength in it. Chase was old, but those hands had been toughened by a lifetime of work. It was almost as if Chase Miller's hands had been toughened in the forging.

"Lord, never thought I'd lay eyes on you again, Shell," Chase said, putting an arm around Morgan's shoulders to walk him across the shop to where two nail barrels served as stools. "Look at the shoulders on you now!" Chase's smile suddenly fell away. "They tell tales about you, boy."

"They're not true, Chase."

"Didn't think they were, son. I read you when you was a boy. I never read the glitter of gold hunger in them eyes of your'n."

"Thanks, Chase. I appreciate that."

"But there's others'll have their eyes lighted up. I don't think it's the idea that you might have done a wrong to the South that angers 'em. It's the idea that the gold was layin' up there and they never knew it. Poor man's anger, Shelter."

"I can understand that. But that's not why I came back. Besides, that gold's long gone. All of it."

"You knew of it?" Chase said.

"I knew. I'm the one who took it, Chase." Then he proceeded to tell the tale, from start to end.

Chase whistled at the end of the story. "I reckon you would've been the only one who could have done that. It would take an old ridge-runner who knew the trails."

"Sometimes, Chase, I find myself wishing I hadn't made it."

"You mean so's it would still be there, waiting?"

"It wouldn't be there," Shelter told him. "There were too many others who knew about it. After war's end there would have been a mad rush to Lookout. Maybe those butchers would have killed each other off instead of . . ."

"Instead of what? Lord, boy, don't tell me

91

you've still been fightin' that war? Huntin' those men!"

Shelter didn't answer. He didn't have to. His blue eyes had that hard, flat look which a hunting man wears. Chase shook his head.

"There was no one else, Chase. That money was for food, blankets, medicine, shoes . . .not for horse ranches."

"Horse ranches?" Chase's eyes were clouded. Abruptly they brightened. "Tennessee Walkers! Say it ain't so, Shelter. Benton Gray was one of them? He was in your outfit?"

"He was cavalry, Chase. But he was one of them. He helped plan it and he helped execute it." The word was bitterly ironic.

"Didn't nobody tell you who he is now?"

"I know who he is. And I know what he was, Chase."

"Lord!" Chase breathed. He stood, rubbing his arms with nervous energy. "If you have your try on Benton Gray, son, they'll hang you from the nearest tree. He's a state senator!"

"He's a killer."

"Same as you'll be if you stalk him, Shelter."

"I'm not going after him to kill him, Chase. I want to show him up, to ruin his career, to get folks to see him for what he is."

Chase Miller was silently thoughtful. "Then you'll have to kill him. The man won't stand for that. He's tasted power and he likes the flavor."

"You don't seem as awed by him as some folks around here."

"Me?" Chase shook his head. "He's a politician. I've seen a few, Shelter. A politician's a man who wants to take your money to save you from poverty. A man who stands aside until the trouble's over and then steps in and tells you what you should have done. Benton Gray—he's worse than some. He's one of them that knows what to do with power."

"Just where is his ranch, Chase?"

"It's the old Potter place, Shell. The house is all new. He's got them white post fences, a race track, all the conveniences. Just like up to Lexington or somethin' . . . I guess that blood gold paid for all of that."

"I guess it did," Shell answered. He rose to leave and Chase rose with him.

"You take it easy, boy. I'd hate to be hearin' sad news about you."

"I'm going to do my best, Chase. Say," he said turning, "just what in hell is going on up toward Lookout? I saw a jumble of tracks, plenty of wagon ruts."

"I don't know, Shelter. Nobody's told me, and I haven't asked. It's Benton Gray's project, whatever it is. I heard John Kramer say they've got a locked gate up there and armed guards. The teamsters are allowed to take their rigs to the gate and then Gray's own men take over."

"Funny way to do business. I'm surprised the teamsters stand for it."

"They stand it or they don't do business. Something Gray's up to he don't want folks to see. What," Chase shrugged, "I couldn't say. I'm not sure I'd want to know, but," he added, eyeing Shelter, "I guess maybe you mean to find out."

"It might help me. Usually there's a reason for secrecy. Often it's because something's not quite legal." Shell wondered, "Benton Gray own all that valley up there now?"

"He does. It's damn near impossible to get to Lookout Mountain from this side. A few months back some kinda artist and writer came down from Washington. Wanted to record the battle site. Gray turned *them* back even."

"Seems that Mister Gray is keeping busy with something, doesn't it? All that traffic ... he spends most of his time up here and not in the capital."

"Puzzlin', ain't it?" Chase commented.

"Right puzzlin'." Shelter stuck out his hand and the blacksmith took it. "Well, Chase, I appreciate the conversation. Glad to find out I've at least one friend left in the hills."

"What about your kin?" Miller asked.

"We're not exactly kissin' kin any longer. I met up with Lavelle Partridge."

"That scum." Chase spat. "He's a dirty one, Shell." The smith grinned. "I was wonderin' what happened to your hands. Noticed they was all bruised up."

"The man's got a hard head, Chase."

"And a hard heart. I've heard of his doin's."

Shelter had planted his hat and was ready to leave. One more question occurred to him, and he asked it.

"Say, Chase, what do you hear about the

Witch Woman?"

"The Witch Woman!" Chase Miller shook his head. "Nothin' no more. You wouldn't of heard, bein' away, but she was taken one night by some drunked-up men, dragged out of her shanty. It was a horrible thing, Shelter, most horrible."

"What happened?"

"I wasn't there, but I heard of it. Everyone did. They took the Witch Woman and hung her upside down on a cross. They they laid kindlin' at her head . . . " Chase's voice was unsteady with remembered horrors. "Then they lit it, Shelter. Set her afire."

"Who did it?"

"They say Jethro Partridge. They say his cows got colic or somethin' and he blamed it on a Witch Woman spell. No one outside the clan would've seen it, of course, but Jethro kinda smiles when she's mentioned, and folks figure it's his way of doin' things. Yes, sir," Chase wagged his head. "It was terrible, Shelter."

"Savage." Shell's lips were compressed tightly. "It's a wonder she survived."

"Survived!" Chase shook his head. "She didn't survive, Shell. I cut her down. Me and John Pennymore. She was roasted and purely dead. Won't nobody be seein' the Witch Woman in the hills no longer."

There was no answer to that, none that came to Shell's mind. He shook Chase's hand again, and Chase noticed his eyes held a deep

95

concern, but Miller figured that the news of the brutal murder had brought that emotion on. Shelter felt no inclination to explain that he had seen the Witch Woman—or her tormented ghost—roaming the hills near the Partridge place.

The sky was clouding up, Shelter noticed as he stepped into the alley behind Miller's shop. He reached for the reins to his buckskin and two arms shot out, going around his neck.

He started to kick out but stopped himself just in time as a pair of full, warm lips met his. He immersed himself in the kiss for a moment, feeling the contours of a woman's body pressed against his demandingly. Then he unhooked her arms and stepped back to study Violet Plank.

"Just wondered if you'd taste as good as you looked," she explained, those blue-violet eyes sparkling.

"Did I?"

"Even better, Mister Morgan."

"I thought we were on opposite sides of the fence, Violet."

"We were. Now I hear you don't even have a side."

"That's what I tried to tell you before."

"I know." She hung her head, sketching a design in the dust of the alley with a bare toe. "I didn't believe you, though. Not until you let me go. Then you went back and got Alexander turned loose from the Partridge boys."

"He didn't seem too pleased. He was more

concerned about that Kentucky rifle."

"He still is," Violet smiled. "But the rest of us is happy to have Junior back. Alexander, that is. He's my baby brother."

Seriously, Shelter told her, "He is now, Violet, but if he keeps running those hills with a gun, you may not have him much longer. He might never have the chance to grow up. You could be shot just as easily, you know?"

"They killed my cousin!" Violet flared up. Her lip trembled and her eyes opened wide with anger. "What are we supposed to do? Run out of the hills?"

"No. But there has to be another way."

"If there is, I never heard it," Violet said. The cloud shadows drifted over them. She trembled slightly, with the sudden coolness, residual anger or perhaps, as her eyes indicated, with something akin to passion.

"Maybe Senator Gray . . . " Shelter began. The man might be compelled to stop trouble in his own district even if it were just for appearances. Violet interrupted him with a harsh laugh.

"That bloody pirate!"

"I thought everyone loved Benton Gray."

"Mebbe all the Partridges. They'd have cause to." A sound nearby caused her to change the flow of conversation. "I come to tell you the Planks are in town, Shelter. I spotted your horse back here — they wouldn't know it. I think you'd be damn well served to ride the back way out of Pikeville."

"I will. I appreciate it, Violet. Really."

She smiled and, surprisingly blushed. She stood there, a sturdy, lushly compact young woman, smoothing out the pattern she had drawn in the dust. But not before Shell had noticed it was a heart with a stick arrow through it.

"There's one other thing, Shelter," she said. "Constable Rains has been keepin' a weather eye out for you over to Whynot. Was I you, I'd stay clear of it."

"I appreciate the warning." Shelter stepped into leather, Violet standing near his buckskin's shoulder, her big blue-violet eyes peering up with wonder. "One more thing, Violet. You must get up toward Lookout now and again. What is Benton Gray up to?"

"I don't get up there no more, Shelter. They ran me off with guns—two big ugly flatlanders. I stay clear. Mebbe, if it were important to you I could shake and slide around some up there."

"I wouldn't want you to get hurt."

"That would trouble you?" she asked.

"Yes." He leaned down and touched her cool cheek with the back of his hand. "It would bother me, Violet."

A pink, blushed rose appeared on her cheek just where he had touched it, and as he turned to ride off, he saw her touching her own hand to her cheek, staring after him.

He found the canyon entrance he wanted

and worked up among the deeply shadowed ridges, through the scattered spruce and oak.

"That's fine, Morgan," he told himself after a while. "Get tangled up with a Plank girl yourself. You know damned well what would happen then."

The wind had picked up, screeching down the long canyons. Shelter turned his collar to the wind and rode on until he found Grizzle Bear Trace and he urged his horse up along the snake-sided trail toward ridgetop. The clouds swelled and gathered, floating through the deep green valleys, and after a time a cannon boomed and Shelter saw the muzzle flash—bone white lightning sparking through the gray of the bloated black clouds. It was raining before he crested out and he could see little in any direction. Someone had drawn an iron gray curtain across the world and now they were flapping it, curling it all around the mountain peaks, the lightning streaking the skies like Death rattling his old white bones.

Shelter had his dark slicker on and his hat drawn low. On the western slopes the wind was a constant, buffeting presence. The rain whipped through the trees, the scent of rain and damp pine nearly overwhelming. The clouds clotted, thickening still more, going to black, the only light the occasional brilliance of lightning.

The conditions were miserable, and showed no sign of improving, but Shelter decided to ride on. He had too many questions unanswered to let a day go by wasted in hiding from weather.

Besides, the weather was a good shield for him. He paused, briefly, beneath a massive pine and then swung the mournful buckskin south, toward the Pikeville road.

It was an hour before he cut the road again. There was no traffic at all in this weather. Muddy water rushed down the ruts the wagon wheels had carved. The valley beyond was screened by rain and low clouds. Shelter hooked his slicker up over his holster, leaving the butt of the Colt free to hand. Then he drifted off the road, riding through the cold slanting steel ribbons of the rain toward Benton Gray's secret.

6.

The day grew colder. The clouds hugged the earth, sifting through the dark forests. Rain dripped from the trees and hammered down from the sky, needling Shelter's face and hands. The buckskin was damp with the rain, cautious as it picked its way across the sodden earth, weaving through the trees.

Shelter had gone five miles toward Lookout, crossing the rain-swollen Hodges Creek, sticking to the rough ground, the cover of the timber. Suddenly he came upon it.

A barbed wire fence, four-strands stapled to new posts. It was strung as taut as piano strings. Cold water dripped from the wire. There was a path worn into the bright green grass on the other side of the fence where guards rode their rounds.

Shelter drifted back into the trees and worked his way northward. The rain had lessened some, and he could see a quarter of a mile across the grassy field beyond the fence. There was no sign of movement, nor of construction.

He drew up abruptly. He was on a rocky outcropping among the pines, and directly below him now was the road, the gate onto the property, and two miserably hunched armed guards.

They stood with their backs to the rain, hats running water. Trying to stay comfortable occupied their minds and they had not seen Shelter. They would have had to lift their faces to the rain in order to pick him out, and they did not seem so inclined.

Shelter backed the buckskin away, leaving it beneath the trees as he worked his way even nearer, down a small ravine alongside the gray, seeping outcropping. Water ran in the ravine, winding among the stones and blackthorn.

The road was awash with mud at this low spot between two stony bluffs and Shelter could see clearly that no vehicles had passed the check point recently. The thick red mud lay in a smooth pool between the feet of the guards.

Looking westward Shelter could see nothing.

No buildings, no machinery of any kind. Nothing. He held his position for nearly an hour. Once a mounted guard making his rounds of the fenceline passed the checkpoint and the three men snarled a surly hello. It was growing even more chill. The rain was like icicles falling against Shell's flesh. The creeks gradually rose and the mudhole inevitably grew.

There was nothing to be learned in this way, and so Shelter started creeping back from his position. He was nearly out of view when he saw the guards jerk upright, and turning his head, Shelter saw the coach laboring down the muddy grade toward the checkpoint.

It was a black, closed coach, the wheels skidding left and then right as the panicked team of bays tried to keep their footing. The driver was solemn, working the reins and brake alternately with great skill and concentration.

As Shelter watched, the coach drew up at the gate with a last little stuttering slide. The driver was a swarthy, dark coated man wearing a derby hat. Shelter didn't make him for an Indian, but maybe a dark Mexican. The gate was swung wide and Shelter heard a voice from inside the coach.

The driver called back with a language as far from Spanish as Shelter had ever heard. He could not identify it. The side curtain of the coach parted just a little and Shell saw a flash of red silk, a shadowed, dark face.

Then the curtain closed and the coach started up again, the horses bucking for traction as they drew the bogged-down coach out of the mudhole and up onto the long road winding across the valley.

Shelter lingered a time longer as the guards latched the gate, hoping their conversation might give him a clue as to who the passenger in that dark coach was. But they said nothing, or if they did, it was drowned out by the drumming of the rain from out of the black skies.

The buckskin lifted its head curiously as Shelter returned. He swept the rain from his saddle and stepped up, riding through the forest in the failing light, the hard wind at his back, water dripping from off the trees, down his collar in icy rivulets.

He stayed a good distance from the road, riding through the monotonous rain, the wind twisting the buckskin's mane into unkempt strands. It was well that he had shunned the road, for they appeared on it, emerging suddenly from the gray web of the storm!

Jethro Partridge with Tom and Lavelle behind him. They rode mules and wore the expression of hunting men — alert, somber, wolfish. Shelter pulled the buckskin up and covered its muzzle with his hand so it would not blow. Pressed against the trees with the screen of rain between them, the Partridges did not see him. They rode steadily on, their eyes flickering to the growth along the side of the trail, their rain damp weapons in hand.

Shelter waited until they rounded the bend in the road, then waited five minutes longer.

Then he walked the buckskin forward, its hoofs soft, silent against the sodden earth and pine needles.

At the corners where the road to his cabin branched northward and the road to Pikeville ran straight ahead, he hesitated. The coach had come up the road past his place, from Whynot or perhaps Thompson's Corners. Looking closer, Shelter could see, even with the wash of rain, that others had used the road recently. The Partridges and five other men. Why? It was a hell of a day for riding unless a man had serious business.

Shelter had planned on not returning to the cabin, but sleeping out when there was a choice made no sense. With some indecision, he turned the buckskin northward toward the farm.

It sat hunched against the rain, gray before the gray background of the day. The huge old pines, towering nearly a hundred feet into the air, swayed in unison before the wind. But they had seen hundreds of storms, many worse, and would likely be there after Shelter himself was only a memory.

Using more caution this time, Shelter circled the house at a distance. Seeing no one, he rode down the slope behind the cabin, coming up from the rear. He led the horse into the dank shambles of a barn, unsaddled and rubbed the horse down. The hay was ancient, moldy, so Shell took the time to pull some grass, working carefully.

Finished, he walked slowly to the house. He knew he was hidden from view, but to reach the door he would have to expose himself. Fortunately the clouds were lower now, and darkness was settling. He doubted any man could see him from across the meadow.

He entered the house cautiously, barring the door behind him. She came into his arms with a tremor and a bucketful of giggles, naked, warm, frothing with delight.

"Shelter."

"Hello, Cassie. I didn't expect to see you so soon," he told the blonde.

"You should have, Cousin," she bubbled. "Recall what I said?"

"I recall it." He let her kiss him, her soft, round arms hugging him tightly.

Night had fallen outside and it was dark in the cabin as well, only a last blade of gray light seeping through a crack in the broken window shutters. Shell held the girl tightly for a moment, letting his hand run down the small of her back and across her smooth white buttocks.

She was breathing rapidly, grinding herself against him. She lifted her face to his and he kissed her—as a cousin.

"Come on, Honey," she encouraged him. But Shelter felt no response to the girl. He could have faked it, but that was no good for either of them. "What is it?" she asked.

Shelter smiled. "Nothing." He wiped back a strand of yellow hair. "You're beautiful, Cassie."

"But it's no good?" she asked, frowning in puzzlement.

"No." Slowly her arms fell away and she walked to the table, sitting at a chair. A gray silhouette, a woman round and naked in the night.

What was it? He couldn't say. Was he still thinking of Elizabeth? Or was it the recent, warm memory of Violet Plank? Maybe it was something more subtle—his body reacting to his mind's warning to stay clear of the Partridges in any shape or form. And Cassie certainly had a nice shape.

Shelter liked his women, and he had had his share. Those deprived years in that Union prison had honed his natural urges to a demanding edge. He liked his women and he liked them ripe and lusty like Cassie Partridge. Yet he was not inclined to be a stud for every thing in skirts, no matter what the record seemed to indicate.

He had simply met a lot of women, and they had found him attractive. He glanced at Cassie, wondering what was going on in her mind. The rain beat down on the roof. A drop of water dripped onto Shell's shoulder.

"Your Pa will skin you, Cassie. Maybe you'd better get back."

"No," she pouted. "Not in that rain, that's for sure. I guess you think I'm the ugliest thing come down the pike, but you're gonna have to look at me a time longer."

Shelter walked to her, put his hands on her

shoulders and kissed her head. He felt her tense under his hands. "I damn sure don't find you ugly, Cassie. No man could." He crouched beside her, smiling up at Cassie Partridge. "I kind of like having my kissin' cousin around, Cassie. I just think we ought to keep it at that."

"All right." She lowered her head impudently. "Kiss me then, Cousin Shell."

Shelter did so, standing to lean to her, his lips brushing her full, parted lips, finding her mouth sweet and moist. Her hands went to his shoulders and she leaned far forward so that her breasts brushed his hand. He felt her tense, felt her kiss grow warmer. Then she sensed that it was not working and she turned her head away.

"Damn!" she breathed. "Damn, damn, damn."

"You know, Cassie. It might be best if you'd head on home rain or not. I saw Jethro and Lavelle down the road. It occurs to me they're probably looking for you. I'd hate to have trouble."

"I bet you could handle it," she replied. She spun saucily and told him, "Anyway, they're not looking for me. Nobody knows I'm gone."

"Then they're looking for me," Shelter said. "And that's even worse."

"They're not, Shelter. I heard Grampa tell the men to leave you alone. That's why I figured it was all right to come up here. I mean, if he's not mad at you any more. Nobody would dare go against Grampa and hurt you."

No? Well somebody had. But who? Who had come sniping the night before? Shelter racked his brains. Not the Planks, and not the Partridges. Benton Gray he had already eliminated, figuring Gray would want a lot more than harassment performed.

Logically then it was not an attempt to kill Shelter. Then what was it? Perhaps, he thought, there was a policy of keeping outsiders away, of making sure no one saw the wagons which rolled into and out of Benton Gray's fortress. A few shots into an unused cabin to get a drifter moving, maybe? It fit everything neatly. And it gave weight to the thought that whatever Benton Gray was up to, it was not strictly legal.

He had taken a risk chasing off those men from Washington. There would undoubtedly be achoes from the capital about that. Therefore, whatever Benton was hiding, the risk was worth whatever trouble the action brought down upon him. Did that mean it was worth killing over? Knowing Gray, undoubtedly.

He thought briefly of the dark men who spoke some foreign tongue. Who they could be and what connection they had with Gray and his project was beyond conjecture. Shelter noticed that Cassie was leaning toward him, watching him closely in the silent night.

"What's the matter, Cousin Shelter? Seems you got problems," she said with soft concern.

He swiveled toward her in the darkness. "I guess maybe I do. Nothing I want to talk about."

He felt her hand on his neck, her fingers twirling a lock of his hair. "I could make them troubles go right away, Honey," she offered.

"No. They wouldn't go away, Cassie. It might delay the thinking on them for a time, but it wouldn't make them go away."

"You never know till you try."

"Maybe I have tried," Shell said. Cassie was silent for a long time.

"You're a strange, serious, beautiful man, Cousin Shell." She stood, clenching her own shoulders. "Brr! It's cold. How about a fire?"

"No fire, Cassie. Not tonight."

"Still thinkin' Jethro and Lavelle are after you?"

"Someone is."

"No fire." She brightened. "But you'll keep me warm, won't you? I'll lay beside you, quiet as a mouse. A warm harmless snuggling. Okay?"

"Okay," he agreed. "We've only got my bed anyway, unless you brought . . . "

"I wasn't thinkin' *that* far ahead, Honey," she laughed.

It was chill. The rain streamed down from out of the cold night, drumming pleasantly against the roof of the cabin.

Shelter rolled into his bed and lifted the blanket for Cassie. She squirmed in quickly snuggling her body against Shell, grateful for the warmth.

"Still . . . cold," her teeth chattered.

"You could put your dress on."

"Wrinkle my best dress! No, sir. Beside, I like this best. I'm warming now." She nuzzled his throat and threw her knee up over his thigh, holding him tightly.

Cassie's hand moved slowly down his chest as she made one more try at stirring his interest. And it did stir him, having this naked, lovely creature next to him in the soundless night, but Shelter avoided telling her how much it stirred him, and she gave it up.

After a few minutes she was asleep, breathing softly, her breath moist on his neck, her hair soft against his cheek. Shelter hugged her more tightly to him and she murmured in her sleep.

"Sorry, Cassie," he whispered to the night. Then he watched the ceiling, listening to the rush of the rain for a long while before sleep overcame him.

Morning was a bright liquid rush of sunlight through the door. Shelter sat up with a start. Cassie, naked still, stood in the open doorway, the sunlight shining in her pale hair, her body burnished by the golden light. A primitive, un-self-conscious thing, she bathed in the warmth, her eyes half closed in animal enjoyment.

A few scattered clouds drifted across the cerulean sky. The meadow was heavy with dew, fresh and green. Quail called from the streambed and a pair of crows cawed and played against the sky.

"I made coffee, sleepy-head," Cassie said. She came to him for a morning kiss. "You sure slept, Cousin Morgan. Maybe that was it—you were just awful tired.

"Could be," Shell agreed. He turned and went to the stove, finding his quart coffee pot boiling over. He poured a cup and walked back to the door, standing beside Cassie, his arm around her.

Maybe it was the sleepiness. She sure looked almighty good this morning. Sunbright blonde hair, full, overripe breasts with taut pink nipples, the slow easy spread of her workmanlike hips, the downy patch of gold fleece between her thighs, the taper of her sturdy legs.

Shell drank his coffee, finding last night's resolve filtering away as his blood began to rise, to heat as the sun warmed the meadow rising higher into the rain fresh sky.

He finished his coffee and stretched out a hand to put the empty cup on the table. As he did so, Cassie stepped into his arms and he took her to him, kissing her mouth, her shoulders.

His hands slid down across the soft flow of her hips and she responded warmly, her lips parting, her eyelids drooping half shut. Shelter turned her toward the bed, reaching back to shut the door.

"Carrie! Damn you!"

The shout came from the yard and Shelter turned, startled to see Carrie Partridge running toward the cabin, her long brown legs flashing in the sunlight. She was shaking a fist as she ran. Cassie was behind Shelter peering over his shoulder, her hands on his back and she moaned fearfully.

"Oh, Lordy. It's Cassie a-comin'."

"Cassie?" Then *she* was Carrie. Shell's head swiveled back toward the yard.

Cassie was covering a lot of real estate and she was nearly to the porch, her bare feet heavy with mud. Carrie—or was it Cassie—shrieked and headed for the interior of the cabin, moaning as she scurried about trying to find a place to hide from her sister's wrath.

"Cassie . . . " Shelter started to speak to the breathless girl, but she bounded up the steps and into the house before Shelter could say anything else. She brushed by him and spotted her sister.

Cassie's eyes opened with indignant menace. "You come to him, knowin' he was mine!"

"Nothin' happened, Cassie! I swear it."

Her sister laughed harshly. "With you like that! Nekked!"

"I swear it, Cassie."

"Swearin' the moon is cheese don't make it so."

Cassie circled the table which was Carrie's refuge and Carrie circled away from her. Cassie suddenly rushed the other way, grabbing at her sister across the table and Carrie shrieked,

113

running toward the door.

"Cassie. Nothing did happen," Shelter said.

"You keep quiet, two-timer!" she snapped. She stalked Carrie, hair hanging, eyes wide, her mouth open. She panted with anger as they circled the table, the chairs like two stalking wrestlers.

"Now, you come to me, you wench," Cassie said in a low growl. "I'll tear your hair out, Carrie."

Carrie's fear had begun to fade, and now anger slowly replaced it. "I ain't 'feard of you, Cassie."

"Then come out and let's have at it, bitch!"

Carrie's eyes opened wide. "You ought not of said that!"

"I'll by-damn say it again. Bitch, bitch!"

"Now you done it." Carrie came forward, her arms low, slightly crouched, her breasts swaying.

"Girls!" Shelter said. Carrie shot him a hard glance.

"Leave us be, Cousin," she said and Shelter shrugged, stepping aside. There was little more dangerous than stepping between two she-cats, and he let them go.

"Now," Carrie said. "Step out in that yard."

"I will. You're hog-right I will!" Cassie turned toward the porch. Suddenly she stopped. "Damned if I'll let you tear my dress," she said.

Then with a deft, cross-armed movement she slipped her dress up and over her head.

She wore nothing underneath and the two sisters faced each other now, naked hellions.

"Now!" Cassie said.

"Now ain't soon enough," Carrie countered. She stepped to the porch ahead of Cassie and started down the steps, but Cassie tripped her and she plummeted forward, landing face first in the wallow of mud the night's rain had produced.

She rose wailing, mud dripping from her face and arms. Cassie laughed, throwing back her head. A hoarse, derisive cackle which was interrupted by a gob of mud Carrie hurled at her sister's face.

Cassie stood stock still for one dreadful moment. Then she spat out the glob of mud from her mouth, wiped her eyes clear and with a sudden banshee shriek she lofted herself through the air.

She collided with Carrie, knocking her back into the mud puddle, Cassie following. A long leg stuck up from the mud, was twisted and fell back. A mud-filmed head raised momentarily and was yanked back by the hair.

They rolled over and over. Mud thick buttocks, breasts, legs and faces in a tangle. Shelter sighed, leaned against the porch upright and watched.

Cassie—or Carrie—leaped up and tried to run, but the mud caused her to lose traction and she tripped over her sister, flopping into the mud again. Cassie had Carrie's hair and Carrie freed herself by reaching back and taking a firm grip on Carrie's breast, squeezing and twisting it.

"Dirty fighting!" Carrie screamed, though through the mud in her mouth it came out like, "Drfitin!" She got off a pretty right hook which slammed Cassie free.

They both came to their feet, grappling. Carrie took her sister by the crotch and neck and tried to heft her to slam her down, but with that footing they both simply toppled over, their resultant curses muffled by mud and anger.

Cassie got on top of her sister and proceeded to stuff her mouth full of mud. Carrie screamed, tossed her head and flailed with arms and legs.

Then Shelter could no longer tell them apart. They were two naked, mud splatted female figures wrestling across the puddle. Up and then down, *splat*. Rolling left then right. Trying to flee, being yanked back by an ankle into the puddle with only an occasional blow actually hitting anything.

Cassie, maybe, swung a hard left at Carrie and missed. Cassie flew over her sister's shoulder. Carrie was elevated briefly, her round ass slapping down hard as she landed and a strange sound came from her throat.

Half a whimper, half a groan. Shelter got ready to wade into the mud. A family tiff was one thing, but if one of them were hurt he would have to stop it immediately.

He started toward them and then heard the other girl making echo-like sounds. It was another puzzled moment before he identified the sounds.

The sounds two giggling girls make when their mouths are filled with mud. They sat there, their shoulders quaking, their gurgling, mud-packed giggling shaking their bodies. They laughed so hard, so long, that their bellies hurt and they could not stand.

Finally they did come to their feet, and they stood together, hugging each other, petting back the mud caked hair, murmuring sisterly apologies.

Arm in arm they skidded and staggered out of the mud and came onto the porch to stand before Shelter. He looked from one to the other. Blue eyes shone behind masks of mud, plastered-down hair hung in brown globs.

"Girls, I hope . . . " he began soberly, but suddenly it overtook him too, and Shelter laughed out loud, leaning back against the house for support. He tried it again, but could only laugh helplessly until the girls started in again, giggling until they had no breath. They held their stomachs.

"No more, no more," Carrie pleaded. Then she looked at her sister and started laughing again herself.

Finally, aching with the fighting and the laughing, they stopped and went off across the meadow to bathe in the creek. Shelter watched them for a minute and then went in to roll up his bed and collect his saddlebags.

They returned clean, teeth chattering, their

ripe flesh studded with goosebumps. They wriggled into their dresses and stood rubbing themselves, hopping up and down. Finally they noticed that Shelter had his saddlebags and rifle in hand.

"You're leavin'!"

"Yes, Cassie."

"I'm Carrie," she interrupted. "But where are you a-headin'?"

"Into Whynot," Shelter told them. "I can't stay here."

"Sure you can. I tol' you, Cousin Shelter, Grampa ain't lookin' for you."

Maybe not, he thought, but someone was. It could be that Jethro Partridge had only said that to set the girls' minds at ease. Anyway, he had the feeling that something was going on in Whynot. It was there all the traffic to Benton Gray's stronghold seemed to originate. Certainly nothing much was known in Pikeville. With Whynot the only other nearby town, it seemed an obvious starting place.

Violet had warned him that Constable Rains was looking for him. But that was a risk that had to be taken. Just what charge Rains might think he had was beyond Shelter's reasoning. Maybe Rains figured he needed none.

"I've got to go," Shelter said. "You two ought to get on back before your Pa scalds your britches."

"No need to go," Cassie said, moving near to Shell. Her fingers flitted around the buttons to his shirt. "Carrie and I could both stay here

118

and keep you warm for as many nights as you decided. Fun beats trouble ever' time, Cousin Shelter."

"It surely does," Shell agreed. "And you know I'm sorely tempted, but I've got some things to do, and my mind can't be changed."

They both went to the door with him, two luscious young things in identical calico dresses. Arms around each other's waists, they watched from the porch as Shelter went to the barn and saddled the buckskin.

They were still watching when, a few minutes later, Shelter rode across the meadow at a walk, aiming northward toward Whynot. He lifted a hand to them and they waved back in unison, bright smiles on their faces.

The day had clouded over again before Shelter had reached Whynot, and he thought, it had a right to. There was a hard rain fixin' to fall.

7.

Whynot hadn't changed appreciably in the ten years since Shelter Morgan had been gone. He peered through the light rain which dappled the street and saw the same faded green hotel where hardly anyone ever stayed, the gray wood of Hanson's Stable, the Ringtail Saloon, the flat roof of the town jail, the Fremont which was once a hotel but which had now been converted to offices downstairs and was the Masonic Lodge upstairs. An unparalleled ugliness was the Fremont's distinctive emblem.

The lower half was done in yellow brick. The work of Winston Fremont, a transplanted New Englander who had not lived to see his landmark completed. The upper story with its narrow, arched windows had been completed roughly with sawn lumber and mismatched shingles.

Even so it was a monumental building for this area.

Shelter eased his buckskin toward the Ringtail. There were six or seven horses standing hipshot, heads bowed in the rain. If there was gossip to be had, it would be had there where men congregated and found their tongues loosened with whiskey.

He stepped in through the door and the gust of wind brought a few heads around to face Shelter. There were three men, obviously teamsters, at one table playing poker, a pair of locals at the bar. Shelter remembered one face but could not put a name to it.

In the corner, sitting quietly over a bottle of wine were two dark, scar-faced men in dark suits. They were not Americans, and as Shell picked up the rusty whispering of their voices he knew that wherever they were from, he had never been there.

There had to be a connection with the dark men Shelter had seen at Gray's stronghold. He walked to the end of the bar nearest their table and caught the barkeep's eye.

"Whiskey," Shell said.

"Thought you boys made your own," the bartender said. At Shelter's hard glance, he explained, "You got the clan face. I heard you was all comin' home to do some fightin'."

"You heard wrong, friend. I'm not here to fight, but only to have a peaceful drink. Since I don't make my own, why don't you hustle yourself over and get me one?" He smiled, but he could see in the smoky mirror that it wasn't a particularly pleasant smile. It wasn't meant to be.

The bartender had the expression of a man who has stepped on a snake and doesn't know if he should tromp down or back up. He looked at the dark, tough looking man, noticing the scar over the eye, the two day beard, those blue-gray eyes. Cold, no-nonsense eyes. He backed up.

The bartender came back, pouring a shot for Shelter. "It's on the house," he said by way of apology. "I didn't mean to rile you. It's a habit I got, trying to read people's faces."

"What do you read on those faces?" Shell asked, nodding toward the two dark men in the corner.

"Damned if I know," the bartender said, scratching his balding head. "Something to do with the Senator. They came in with some others. Some kinda high mucky-muck wearin' a red sash like a lady. But what this is all about I couldn't tell you. I don't speak their lingo, so I never asked 'em. And I got the feelin' they're the kind that wouldn't answer you anyway."

"Think something's up?"

The bartender shrugged and shined the bar with a lazy, flicking cloth. "Somethin's always up, mister. What, I suppose it's best not to know."

Shell turned his back to the bar and hooked his boot heel over the rail. Someone had drawn to a flush at the card table and taken the pot with a lot of whooping and grumping. The door opened again and Shelter glanced that way.

A kid of twenty or so started in the door grinning. He hesitated, looking directly at Shell for a long second before his glance fell away. Then he backed out, closing the door again.

It smelled like trouble. As casually as he could, Shelter commented, "Looks like the kid prefers the rain."

"Doug? He drinks on duty sometimes, but he ain't supposed to. Must've changed his mind."

"He the constable?" Shelter asked innocently.

"Deputy."

The bartender moved down the line to draw a beer for the old-timer with the chin whiskers. Shelter finished his drink without apparent haste and started for the door.

That deputy, he would bet, was on the run for Rains right now. Glancing around the room once more, he noticed with surprise that the two dark men were gone. There was a back door, of course, for loading and dumping trash, but Shelter hadn't even seen them rise. It sent a chill up his spine to think of those big, scarred men moving like cats on soft feet.

The rain blew into Shelter's face as he opened the door. The rain was steady now, hard. He could barely make out the lights of the Fremont across the street.

He walked to the tie rail and stopped cold. The buckskin was gone.

Gone, and he knew he was in trouble. From down the street he heard a sound near the constable's office, and he saw the silhouettes of two men briefly before a lighted window.

Shelter turned on his heel and entered the alley on his left, striding quickly through the rain. He heard feet clattering on the boardwalk in front of the Ringtail and he kept moving, losing himself in the shadows and the rain.

He came around the corner, the mud to his ankles. He was concentrating on what might be behind him and not what was ahead of him, and the silver flash of the knife blade barely missed his throat.

Shelter ducked and kicked out. The two dark men were there, facing him, knives carried low. Shelter started to draw, but the slicker hampered him and one of them lunged.

Shelter rolled aside, felt his Colt slapped from his hand and felt the bulk of the man drive into his shoulder.

He went down, rolling in the cold mud and

the second thug hurled himself at Shelter. Shell got his feet lifted and his legs were jarred as the dark man's body met his boot heels. He grunted and went down, Shelter twisting aside as the first man again tried it with his blade.

Shelter reached down, pawed for his Colt, but there wasn't time. They were both up, on him like cats. Shell felt the cold rain wash over him, felt the chill of the wind and then as one of them feinted and lunged, a hot sensation which flooded his side with pain.

Angrily he slammed a forearm against the man's throat, and he grunted, clutching at a battered windpipe. Shell kicked out and knocked the knife free, but the second one was all over him, hooking an arm around Shelter's neck as he tried to drive the silver blade of his knife into Shelter's back.

Shell drove back with a fist into the thug's groin then, as that slacked the grip, he tore at the dark man's hair, getting a good hold. He ducked, flipped the attacker and the man slammed into the mud on his back. He was to his feet instantly and he drove at Shell.

Shelter ducked and the thug went over. Then there was something hard and razor sharp. Shell's hand found the other knife and he swung up and around with it as the foreigner made his charge.

Shell drove it up hard, a savage anger behind the blade. He twisted up from his ankles, using his thighs, back and shoulders and he drove the blade to the hilt, feeling the warm gush of hot blood against his fist. The attacker staggered back, holding the knife which was deep in his abdomen, just below the breast bone.

He growled a low, foreign curse and sagged to the mud where he sat, the life leaking out of him.

Shelter whirled around, hearing voices from the street. He saw the flash of lanternlight and he staggered on, holding his side to staunch the flow of blood. He rounded the corner, the pursuit hot behind him, and stumbled into the haunch of his horse.

Shelter blinked through the pain and the film of cold rain uncertainly. Then he focused on the horse and dragged himself up.

They had taken the horse. Therefore they had planned to execute him. The idea seemed faintly humorous, and he realized that he was getting giddy with the loss of blood.

A shout and a following muzzle flash brought him out of it sharply. A bullet thudded into the siding of the building behind him and Shelter hunched low across the withers of the buckskin, raking it with his heels.

The buckskin was at a dead run in four strides, slopping through the mud and the bitter rain into the shadows beyond Whynot. Looking back Shelter saw a progression of winking red eyes veiled thinly by the storm, and he realized without giving it any significance that they were firing at him.

The horse slowed at the freshet beyond town, shying from the white water. It waited uncertainly for a hand to guide it. There was none.

Shelter clung to the pommel of his saddle with both hands, his mind tangled with colorful, meaningless threads of thought.

He knew he was on horseback, knew it was raining. He opened his eyes and peered at the creature beneath him, but it seemed to be a horned, scaly beast of some kind, and he did not want to look at it.

There was hot life seeping from a chasm-like point of pain in his side. Hot life which oozed out from the wound and was washed away in the torrent of sound, the wash of icy drumming which was the rain. The horse wandered through the night and Shelter, unaware of direction or danger, clung to the saddle, holding to it as if it were the source of life itself.

The rain roared down.

The rain roared down and the skirt rustled near him. The rain bludgeoned the earth tearing leaves from the cottonwoods, flooding the gorges with whitewater rapids and the man barked a laugh.

Shelter clung to the brass rail of the bed and the roar of rain died away from his ears and he sat suddenly upright, pain scalding his side.

"You better take it easy now, Shelter," she said.

He let his head sag back. It throbbed and

hammered. He felt a cool hand on his brow and through the rain he saw Violet Plank smiling worriedly at him. He closed his eyes and let the storm swallow him.

When he awoke again things were a little clearer. He was in a bed, shirtless, a quilt over him. There was a bandage around his waist, very tightly wound. The room was small, roughly built but neat. Violet was not there, but looking up Shelter saw the kid, Alexander.

He looked at Shell, grunted dispassionately and rose, walking out into another room where beans and ham hocks were cooking. The smell grabbed at Shelter's stomach.

In a minute she was there, wearing a blue gingham dress, her hair in a single braid. She came to where Shelter lay and sat on the bed beside him, smoothing her skirt.

"Hello, Shelter."

"Violet." He looked around. "Is this your house?"

"It is. You're in my bed. Alexander found you out on Twelve Post Road."

"Twelve Post!" That was a hell of a long way from Whynot and from the ranch. "There was a fight," he told her.

"I saw."

"You're the doctor?" he asked.

"You think any other Plank would lift a finger to help you?"

He shook his head. He studied her fine-boned face, those compelling eyes. He knew by the dress, by the scent of jasmine, that she had fixed herself up for him. Her smile was shy, her eyes bold.

"I appreciate it, Violet."

"Who done it to you, Shelter? Was it the Partridges?"

"No. Two men I never saw before. Dark, scarred men."

"Really!" She wore a look of bafflement. "I wouldn't think Benton Gray would turn those Turks loose in town."

"Turks?"

"That's what they are. They're the ones that have business with Senator Gray. Some kind of business."

"You're sure?" Turks, were they? What was there to be made out of that? "I smell something mighty good cooking."

"Beans and hocks is all," she shrugged. "Want some? I've cornbread too. Buttermilk."

"I feel like I haven't eaten for days," Shell told her.

"You haven't. You've been right here three days, Shelter. I expect you have a right to be hungry."

She rose, started to bend over him to kiss him, then only straightened his pillow. When she stood up again, Shelter saw the reason for her change of heart.

He stood in the doorway, a straight whip of a man, perhaps sixty years old with a white beard and biting blue-violet eyes. "He alive still?" the old man cracked.

"Still is, Pa."

"Get him some vittles then, Vi. Let's get this Partridge well and get him out of here."

"Yes, Pa." She bowed from the neck and scuttled by her father, holding her skirt up.

The old man walked nearer the bed, a Spencer rifle in his gnarled fists. This was Mason Plank, the head of the clan A rough and sour mountain man with a fierce hatred for flatlanders, revenuers and Partridges.

"I'm not a Partridge, Mister Plank. I'm . . ."

"I know who you are, sonny! Shelter Morgan. Your Pa was second cousin to Leo Corbett. Corbett's a Partridge cousin. That makes you a Partridge to me!"

"It doesn't to the Partridges," Shell said.

The old man looked at him sharply. There was a hint of a smile, but it was gone like a vagrant wind. Shelter noticed that at all times the man stood far enough away that Shelter could not grab for his rifle if he were so inclined.

"Turks get ye?" Plank asked.

"Yes, sir."

"Why?" he asked; squinting up his eyes querulously. "Thought you Partridges was on Benton Gray's side."

"Side? The Partridges may be—to tell you the truth, I don't know who's on whose side, what in hell is going on up here. One thing I do know. Any side Benton Gray is on, I'm across the fence."

"You say that strong, boy."

"I mean it strong."

He rubbed his chin. "I near b'lieve ye, son."

"You can believe it, Mister Plank. As for the feud, the rest of it, I don't care a whit. But Benton Gray — that's another story."

"You could be a-lyin'."

"Could be. But I'm not. Look, I know you lost a boy to Jethro Partridge . . . "

"You know why?" Plank asked.

"Yes. Polly Partridge . . . "

"Didn't have a damned thing to do with Aaron getting that Partridge girl with foal. Hell, Morgan, don't you see — that happened months ago?"

"She is far along. I wondered . . . "

"Ye didn't wonder far enough. Was it over that, Jethro would've seen to Aaron quick. Likely he just would've had 'em married and shunned from the hills. Same as me. No, sir." He shook his white head, "Aaron was killed because he was on Senator Gray's property. He was killed because he seen what they was up to."

"And just what is that?" Shell asked.

"Don't know. Hoped you'd tell me."

"I have no idea in the world."

"Then what's Gray after you for?" Plank wanted to know.

"Something that happened a long time back. It's a long story."

"Tell me about it."

Violet had come into the room with a smoking platter. She sat it aside and propped Shelter up before giving him the dish.

131

"It is a long story, Mister Plank. And it doesn't have anything to do with Aaron."

"So tell me anyway. It's rainin' and my fiddle's broke. I got the time. Talk and eat."

Shelter nodded. He tasted the beans first, then had a wedge of hot buttered cornbread washed down with buttermilk. Slowly he began, talking between bites and around the food.

When he was through with the telling, his plate was empty and Violet took it away, returning with a cup of coffee heavily flavored with chickory and given sting by a shot of moonshine.

Mason Plank was silently thoughtful and finally he said, "It figures, I 'spect. Al'ays thought somethin' was wrong with that Benton Gray. They is a way about the man. He's a skulker and a stomper inside. Ye can see it behind them eyes.

"And the gold—that ain't a new story. It's been goin' around here . . . oh, I'd say since shortly after Gray moved back up into the hills, that there was gold hidden up there. Gets folks excited." Mason Plank turned his head and spat with great precision into the far corner.

"But I take it it didn't get you excited?"

"Me? Hell, boy. I heard gold stories all my life. Folks go runnin' here and there diggin' holes. Killin' each other likely. The way I figure it is I'm hearin' it twice-hand, third-hand. Either the gold ain't there or the man who heard the tale fust-hand got it already."

132

"Recall the Witch Woman, Pa?" Violet put in. Mason Plank frowned and spat again.

"Yeees, and that was another sorry spectacle. Folks had the notion the old she-witch had a trunk of pirate gold. Like to tore her place apart root and stone after Jethro burned her up."

"Was it Jethro?" Shelter asked.

"Who else! Who else we got so be-damned dirty and vicious in these hills? Yeees, it were him for a certainty."

"Well," Shelter told him, "you're right about the gold. It's long gone. I know it and Benton Gray knows it."

"Don't stop fools from believin'," Plank snorted.

"You mean Jethro Partridge."

"I do, for a fact. The old buzzard is skulking around the mountain, jest a-lookin' and a listenin'. He's dead certain Benton Gray has the gold locked up. That's what they say all the work up there is."

"You don't think so."

"Not hardly. Fust thing if they was minin', they got no miners. And I know they ain't no gold around here unless it's been toted in like that you was talkin' of. Number two," he said touching another finger, "it ain't no toted-in gold."

"You know it for a fact?"

"I know it by the light of the logic God gave me, boy. How many wagons you reckon you'd need to carry off a million in gold?"

133

"One."

"Keerect. Mebbe two. Benton Gray's got ten on the road a day. He guards them wagons like they was gold, but they ain't. Can't be."

"I agree with you. But is it possible there's gold buried deep in one of those tunnels up there. Maybe a shaft blown up by cannon fire or powder flash?"

"Could be." Plank scratched his whiskered chin. "Those hills, especially Lookout are tunneled up like nothin' you ever saw. Did it durin' the war, and it's possible. But I double-doubt it."

"Why?"

"Reasonin' agin, son. If he's diggin', why take the tailings away by wagon? No sense at all to that."

"So we're back where we started from," Shelter said. He handed Violet the empty cup and refused a second. The white lightning was kicking up in his stomach.

"Aaron, he knew, I b'lieve," Plank said. "He told me he had seen somethin' up there. Somethin' strange."

"But he didn't get around to telling you?"

"No. Said he would, but first he wanted to talk with somebody about it."

"Partridge?" Shell suggested.

"I doubt it, but I don't know. Don't seem likely, circumstances considered. Mebbe Sheriff Dantley up to the county seat. He's a straight lawman. Not like Rains who's a Plank by marriage but a Gray man by the way he tilts."

134

"I've heard of Dantley. He tried to arrest Lavelle Partridge, didn't he?"

"He did. And a sorry damn mess that was. Lila Hendrikson was the little girl's name. Lavelle swears he didn't do it, but anyone who knows him knows he likely did. He's nasty with women, Morgan. Real nasty. Benton Gray plucked him out of that particular fire. Gray told him flat to stay out of the hills, but Dantley he stands tall. He told Benton Gray that he was an elected official just like Gray and he would damned well do his job for the folks that hired him. All the same," Plank mused, "you don't see Dantley in the hills much."

Oddly Shelter had grown closer to this hill country patriarch in an hour than he had been to his own blood relation, Jethro Partridge. Of course there was no connection between how well you liked a man and blood ties; but in the hills blood was trust, always had been and probably would be until some day some magician figured out a way to bring pictures of how things were outside the hills in.

There was a dignity, a rough honesty about Mason Plank, and he could see how he had fathered such a daughter. Violet was strong mentally and physically, loyal but not closed-minded. He liked Mason Plank . . . and he liked his daughter.

"There's only one way to find out what's going on up on the Gray place," Shelter said finally. "And I'll be doing it as soon as I'm able."

"You're goin' callin'?" Plank asked.

"Yes. That's where the answers are."

"You mind your step, boy. I'd like to see Gray brought down as much as anyone, on account of Aaron. I figure the senator's responsible for that. I'd hate to see you end up like Aaron. Like your Pa, for that matter."

Shelter frowned and shook his head. "What do you mean—like my Pa?"

"Why don't *you* know? Hell, boy folks around here all figger your Pa was murdered."

Murdered? "He had a heart attack," Shelter said quickly.

"I know." Mason Plank stood heavily. "But there's different sorts of heart attacks, son. Some is nature's way, some man's way. I don't know who done it, nobody does, I guess. But . . . hell, maybe there's nothin' to it."

He retracted what he had said, but he did it too hastily, too thinly. Doubt lingered in the air and Shelter felt it tumble through his mind. *Pa murdered*?

Had he kept that secret from his son at his dying moment? Shelter shook his head. The conception was too new, too strong. The moonshine was working in his blood, the weariness returning.

He yawned despite himself and saw Violet smiling at him through the purple haze between them. He yawned again and closed his eyes. When he did so, she was gone and the room was clothed in darkness.

He tried to fight the sleep he felt dragging

him down into a soft, fuzzy hole, but he could not despite the colliding thoughts, the problems which needed resolution, the questions which hung demandingly in the deep recesses of thought.

Giving it up he closed his eyes again and drew the quilt up under his chin, his battered body relaxing under the influences of warmth, food and whiskey. It was hours later, the hesitant silver moon peering in his window when Shelter awakened suddenly, his heart hammering. She was there in the window for just an instant. When he blinked she was gone, and when he hobbled to the window he could not see her against the shadows, the deep forest.

The Witch Woman, come a-prowlin'. Shelter crawled back into bed, shaking his head as if that would clear it all up somehow. Was it caused by the whiskey, by sleep? Somehow he knew it to be real, and that thought was uncomfortable. He closed his eyes and slept, walking through a tangled dream filled with witches and gold, blood and dark-faced demons. Over it all a thundering, crimson rain fell until the dream was washed away and deep, hard-earned sleep came.

8.

Morning brought a moving breeze which fluttered the shutters and rattled the leaves in the big oaks beyond the house. Shelter sat up gingerly, feeling a dull ache in his skull, a gnawing pain in his side.

The house was quiet, the light through the window gray and dull. He unwound the bandage around his waist, wincing as he pulled scab free.

The wound was clean, but jagged and still leaking blood. The knife had taken him five inches above the hip bone and slashed outward, slicing a good chunk of meat away.

The door creaked open and Shell glanced up from his bed to see Violet, her hair brushed and ribboned, standing watching. She held a pot of coffee and a plate where three eggs nudged some smoking hot grits.

"You shouldn't have taken that off," she reprimanded him.

"I wanted to have a look at it. You did a nice job on it."

She blushed faintly, nodded and came to the bed, putting the pot and platter down on the bedside table which was a section of oak log with the drawer space carved out.

She lifted the bandages herself, and asking, went to the far corner where a fresh, tattered sheet lay. She tore it into strips as Shelter helped himself to coffee, eggs and grits.

"Make a good job of it, Violet," he told the girl as she wound him up once more with bandaging. "It'll be a time before I get that one changed."

"No it won't, I'll ... " she stopped and looked at him, her fingers hovering motionlessly above the knot she was tying. "What do you mean, Shelter?" she asked suspiciously.

"I'll be riding today."

She laughed. "You can't! Besides," she added, "it's due to rain."

"All the better for this ride," he said. He drank his coffee, watching her troubled expression, the wariness in those blue-violet eyes.

"What are you going on about, Shell? You can't mean . . . " she laughed again as if it were an insane notion.

"I'm riding to Benton Gray's. Up to Lookout."

"Like this? You can't make it!"

"I'll make it."

"You need rest!" She waved a futile hand toward the window. "For God's sake, it'll rain."

"I've ridden in the rain before, Violet," he said with a faint smile. The concern built in her eyes, finally she nodded.

"Then I'm going too," she said.

"Like hell you are."

"Like hell I'm not, Shelter Morgan!" she insisted. "Who's going to take care of you. You prob'ly don't remember half of the trails, how the creeks lie, how to get into Gray's property now, where his guards are. I know all of that!"

Shelter couldn't fault her logic, but she had no stake in this. It was fine for him to take the risk; it was his life. But he had no wish to involve this young woman in it. He told her so.

"That's fine," she replied sharply. "You have a stake, I don't. The hell I don't, Shelter! I've got a stake in you!"

He gave up the argument. Mason Plank would have something to say about his daughter traipsing around the hills with a crazy Morgan boy. He would let her father handle it.

In the meantime he relaxed, letting his breakfast settle. Violet sat beside his bed in a rocker. She hummed softly, her eyes on the window where a soft rain had begun to draw quicksilver patterns on the panes.

The heat from the fireplace in the other room drifted in, and beneath the quilts, the woman humming gently at his side, Shelter again fell to sleep. When he awoke it was cold, pitch dark and he cursed himself for wasting the day.

The fuzziness was gone from his mind and the headache had relinquished its iron grip. He swung from the bed, moving carefully to avoid ripping his side open again. He was touched by dizziness briefly as he stood, but he shook it off and found his boots and shirt. His slicker was draped over a chair and his Winchester, cleaned and oiled, rested against the wall.

His holster was empty and it took him a minute to remember losing it in the mud of the Whynot alley. He strapped the gunbelt on anyway. The cartridges in the loops were .44s, the same caliber his rifle used.

He open the door a crack, slicker over his arm, and peered out cautiously. Mason Plank had been friendly enough, but there were always the possibilities that the old man had been pretending to draw Shell out or that the other clan members had changed his mind. He didn't wish to find out suddenly.

Three figures slept near the banked fire. One of them twitched an arm, yawned audibly and drew the blanket up around his ears. Shelter crossed the dark room on cat feet.

He could hear the murmuring of soft rain outside and he opened the door quietly, letting in an inevitable gust of cool wind, but he was through the door, closing it softly before the searching fingers of the damp breeze alerted their drowsing senses.

Shelter shrugged into his dark slicker, tugged his hat low and started off toward the lean-to stable. He had taken three steps when he halted, turned and whispered, "Good-bye, Violet."

The buckskin lifted its head with hopeful curiosity and Shelter rubbed its neck. He reached for his saddle and blanket and rigged his buckskin. The bit he warmed against his stomach before slipping it into the buckskin's mouth.

Shelter slipped the rifle into the boot and had half-stepped up into leather when he heard the rushing footsteps behind him. He turned, crouching automatically, his fists clenched before he recognized the shadowy figure.

"Violet!"

"Thought you could sneak off, did you?"

He watched as she led a star-faced roan out to saddle and he told her. "You go on back into the house. I told you you're not going."

She smoothed her saddle blanket and threw her saddle over the roan's back with amazing ease. "You want me to yell, Shelter? I could tell bad stories, you know."

"You'd lie?"

"Damn right, Mister Morgan. I'd tear my

142

shirt off and raise weepin' hell."

He nodded, studying her face. The roof of the lean-to cast a dark shadow across her. The gray ghost of a rain dribbled down. "I believe you would," he said.

"Let's ride then," Violet said. She kneed her roan, forcing out the extra air the reluctant horse was holding in, tightened her cinch and swung up.

Shelter shook his head. He walked his buckskin out and stepped into the stirrup, throwing a long leg over. Violet was smiling and he shook his head heavily. "You're a mean woman, Violet Plank."

"That's right again. Here." She fished into the pocket of the leather jacket she wore and handed him a pistol. "I know you lost yours. This is a Smith & Wesson. It's a .44, and I guess that's what matters. It's Pa's," she added. "If you see him a-comin', you'd best shuck it."

"That I will do," Shelter agreed.

He swung his horse southward then through the rain, and Violet rode silently beside him. A faint moon drifted overhead, glinting intermittently between the silver-edged clouds. The rain was light, hardly bothersome, but the ground was sodden, the wind harsh through the pines.

Toward midnight the wind stopped and the moon yawned, stretched silver arms and emerged from the cloud banks, shining its face across the dark countryside.

"If we can ride to Weaver Creek, bypass

the falls and get over Knob Rock, we should be down behind the Gray place at sunup. That's the only stretch they don't patrol regular, Shelter, though I expect they're supposed to."

"That's the long way around," Shell observed.

"They's a lot of short ways if you don't mind gettin' shot," Violet responded.

Shelter grinned at her and nodded surrender. He let her lead through the thickets and rabbit runs. The moon glistened on water which seeped in sheets from the rock faces. They had climbed several hundred feet now, and they could overlook the countryside from Whynot to Pikeville and up to Lookout where the great mountain shone an eerie blue beneath a mantle of flat-bottomed cloud.

They walked a slick, narrow trail up to the outcropping which half circled Knob Rock. There was a place, much higher up, where an acre of valley was dusted with grass and cedar. There was a deep spring bubbling forth there, and along the base of the rock walls you could still see places where ancient Indians had scratched their prayers, their history or their dreams into the stone. Wishes and prayers drawn in lines and squiggles, unintelligible, but outlasting most wishes. They were silent testimony to the common yearnings of all mankind.

They crested the trail and watched the long valley where white fences criss-crossed a silver-green field. A huge white house with red tile roofing sat up on a small knoll in the exact center of the ranch.

"There it is. What gold will buy," Violet said. Her roan blew and she patted it. "I don't know how a man could sneak up on it, though. There's nothing but empty space all around for hundreds of yards."

Shelter was silent. He was thinking the very same thought. Benton Gray was still a soldier at heart, perhaps. His command post on a hillrise surrounded by flat grassland, patrolled by armed sentries.

"That will be tricky," he said. "Maybe I won't have to take him there, though."

"Where then?" Violet asked.

"I don't know, but he's got to come out sometime, doesn't he?"

Shelter stepped down and helped Violet from her horse. The rain had stopped so he stripped off his slicker. He loosened the cinches and let the horses tug at some long grass.

He stood then, hands on hips, studying the set-up. Violet was close beside him and he felt her hip nudge his thigh. He turned to her and her eyes were moonbright. Her straight white teeth behind full lips caught the moonlight as well, as her mouth parted.

"There's no point in riding any farther tonight," she said. She moved nearer, her breasts brushing his chest as her head tilted back.

"No sense at all," Shelter agreed.

He put his arms around her waist and kissed her slowly. Her hair was damp with the rain, but beneath that shirt she was warm. Without

145

saying a word he took his slicker from the saddle and spread it back in the sheltered cut beside the road.

When he straightened up from that task he saw the moonlight gleaming on her bare flesh. She had stripped and stood there now with moonfire in her eyes, bathed in quantities of moondrops as the light from that distant sphere caught the spattering of raindrops on her body.

"Cold for this, isn't it?" Shelter asked.

"Join me and see," Violet challenged.

She watched with growing interest as he kicked off his boots, stripped his shirt off and then dropped his trousers.

"You don't look all that cold," she teased. Then she walked to him, pressing the warmth of her body to him and the night seemed no longer chill.

Shelter took their blankets from their rolls and Violet lay back, her eyes glittering up at him as he got down next to her, drawing the blankets over them.

It was cool. A little water had gotten onto the groundsheet and it stung their naked flesh with an icy brand, but the blankets were warm and their body heat built as Shelter kissed Violet's lips, her breasts and cold, taut nipples, her abdomen beneath the tent of the blankets.

The clouds drifted over, turning out the light of the moon and they were alone in a tangle of arms and legs, the cold world locked away by their warmth.

Violet was on her back, Shelter propped up beside her, and her hand dipped between his legs, fondling his growing erection. She swept it across her soft abdomen, the touch of flesh on flesh intense, maddening.

Slowly he rolled toward her and he took her in his arms as she positioned him before her warmth. He slid into her, watching the smile on her face deepen, become nearly mystic.

Violet began to pitch and roll and they clung together. She was a living flame beneath him, sparking with sensuality, enveloping him in fiery need.

Her legs went around his waist and she clung to him as if he were all that stood between her and emptiness. Then she began to flood with her own warmth and Shelter, feeling it, intensified his swaying magic. The rain began again, but they hardly cared. Shelter pulled the blanket over their heads and they sparred and then the sparring became a raging battle, each of them driving against the other, twisting, grappling as the rain fell down, as Shelter felt Violet flare up, wriggle and shudder as the flame of her own body incinerated her.

Violet was warm, godawful warm. The blankets steamed. A dull sweetness began in her loins, rising in hot rivulets to her breasts where her nipples tingled beneath Shelter's lips.

Then the sweetness was melancholy —

short-lived, a hunger, an explosion in turn. Shelter was hard against her, the cords of his muscles flexing and slacking. She ran her fingers across his shoulders, feeling those muscles, the hard corduroy of the woven flesh beneath his taut skin. His hips swayed against her, driving deeply, and his breath was warm against her flesh as he tensed, and she felt his need transforming to savage wanting. He clawed at her, and the rough hands brought a second, even sweeter, more tortuous need to her body and they swam together through a pagan love dance until all of the knots of their body were undone and they lay panting beneath the blankets, the rain washing down with gentle warmth.

They stayed beside each other, huddled against the cold until the constant rain began to drift trickles of run-off into the bed and they knew it was no good.

"We'll have to get on our feet," Shelter said with regret. He kissed her eyelids, the damp tip of her freckled nose.

"Can we do it that way?" she asked without opening her eyes.

"We can," Shell smiled, "but it's not what I meant. The footing's no good for that anyway."

She barked a short laugh and placed her twining arms around Shelter's neck, craning her neck to kiss him which she did with a satisfied little hum.

"You're a nice man, Shelter Morgan. Nice

to me."

"I had my reasons," he replied.

"I'll bet you did."

She kissed him again and Shelter relaxed against her for one moment, reluctant to rise. He felt her lips against his, the softness of her flesh and then the sudden violence.

The blankets were drawn tight around them, hands grabbed hold of Shelter's shoulders and a fist slammed against the side of his skull, turning the fireworks on. He tried to struggle but the blankets were like a cocoon. They were rolled over twice and then Shelter felt the sharp binding of ropes.

They lay there, face to face, tied in the roll of blankets, the cold rain in their faces.

"Now ain't that a pretty package for ye," Jethro Partridge said, chuckling without humor. The clan chief stood over them, a viciously grinning Lavelle beside him. Two more men stood away, holding the mules.

"Didn't hear us with the rain, did ye, Morgan? With the sloppity sounds you was makin' your ownself? A pretty package," the old man said, squatting down. "Two little love-birds in their little nest. One a Morgan, the other a hog-suckin' Plank!"

Shelter said nothing. This was no time to rile the man with clever remarks. They had them trussed and bundled like old laundry. The rain washed down across Shelter's face. Violet's quickened breath was against his cheek.

149

"What do you want, Jethro?"

"What do I want? What in hell you think I want, boy? I want that damned gold cache of your'n." He stood and eared back the hammer of his Sharps rifle. "And you're takin' me to it or you'll never take anyone anywhere again."

Shelter nodded with slow understanding. The man was gold-hungry. To tell him there was no gold would be to take that rifle butt in the teeth, or worse, a quick deadly message from the other end of that Sharps, the working end.

"Let the girl go then," Morgan said evenly.

"The hell you say!" Jethro laughed harshly. "Not likely, boy."

"Why not? She can't help you any."

"She can hurt me, boy. She can hurt me. No," he said wagging his bearded chin. "I'll not play your rules. We'll play mine. She comes along and if you don't turn that gold over to me, she don't come back.

"Think on that, Morgan. Think on it, boy. She ain't nothin' to me, but a damnable Plank. You seem to have a fondness for her," he added with a dirty little smile.

"All right." Shelter agreed. There was nothing else to do. To refuse now would mean a bullet for himself and Violet in all likelihood. At least agreement would get him on his feet where he would have a chance, however slim, against four men.

But this could not end well. Jethro Partridge

was a killing man. And when he found no gold, that instinct would boil to the surface like a raging hell. Shelter looked to Violet, but he saw only fear in her eyes. She trembled as they untied her, her face a death mask.

Sunrise was coloring the eastern skies beneath the layer of clouds. Birds took wing through the clearing skies and bands of gold fanned out across the valley below. A beautiful, hopeful dawning for a day which would end in tragedy.

9.

They were untied and dressed, with Lavelle Partridge staring with slobbery, toothy eyes at Violet Plank. Tom and Bob Partridge sat their mules, rifles across the saddles, watching Shelter's every movement as he dressed in the cold morning light and stepped into the saddle of his buckskin. Shelter was glad to notice that Duncan Corbett had not come along on this.

His boots were tied to the stirrups, his hands

to the saddlehorn. Violet was tied similarly, Lavelle taking a long time with the ropes.

"Ye can play with her later!" Jethro snapped and Lavelle glanced up wolfishly. His face was still discolored and lumpy from the fight with Shelter.

Shell glanced at him, caught the seething hatred in his eyes and decided that they were exactly that—playthings for Lavelle after this was done. One to be plowed and one to be battered. Like a big ugly, malevolent child Lavelle stepped into the saddle of his mule, his eyes glittering with mixed, gleefully evil emotion.

They rode with the dawn on their left shoulders, the returning storm on their right. The long valley was cut by freshets, glittering in the new sunlight. Ahead Lookout Mountain scowled through a screen of clouds.

"What about Gray?" Shelter asked. "He won't like this much, will he?"

"He won't bother us. We've rid plenty of fence for the senator."

"I thought this was all secret stuff."

"It's a secret to some, to some it ain't. Me, I got a handle on it."

"So did Aaron Plank, I hear."

Jethro glanced sharply at Shelter, the lines around his eyes deepening with sour amusement.

"I guess he did," Jethro replied.

"Is that why you killed him for the senator?" Shell asked.

"That's why," Jethro admitted with a readiness which surprised Shelter until he considered that Jethro had no idea of letting Shelter or Violet get out of this alive enough to carry the word to Sheriff Dantley or anyone else.

"Jethro," Tom said, lifting his chin.

The old man saw them as well. Guards wearing white slickers strung out in a line across the grass, angling toward them.

"Take it easy," Jethro advised them. He lifted a hand toward the guards. The gesture was unanswered. The men veered toward the Partridge group.

Shelter felt his hopes rise, twist, fall away. He would be worse off—if that was possible —with Benton Gray than with Jethro. Still, if the two outfits tangled, there might be a chance for Shelter and Violet to somehow slip away.

"They're comin' on," Bob Partridge said. He drew back the hammer on his rifle.

"Set easy," Jethro said. "Who is that, Tom?"

"Dave Corson," Lavelle said, recognizing the lead guard.

Jethro stood in his stirrups and shouted, "Ho, Dave!"

The guard's voice reached them across the distance and Shelter saw a hand go up.

"Ho, Jethro! Where you riding?"

"South corner," Jethro called back. There was a moment's hesitation and then the patrol swung off. Jethro grinned, a small expression of triumph.

154

Lavelle turned in his saddle to watch the guards until they were gone over the far grassy knolls. Then he settled into leather, alternately scowling at Shell and mentally undressing Violet.

They had two hours of good bright sunshine in which they drew nearer to the massive bulk of Lookout. Then the clouds let go once more, the rain running toward them across the valley in a convoluted curtain.

"Here it comes," Lavelle shouted. "Break out the raincoats."

Shelter's slicker was placed over Violet's shoulders, and he was left to ride through the rain in only his cotton shirt and jeans. The rain had a deal of wind behind it and as they began to climb the long winding trail to Lookout, the wind fussed and shrieked at them from out of the stony canyons.

"Look familiar, Morgan?" Jethro asked, riding close to Shelter.

The great wedge of blue-gray stone swam through the rain. Lookout stood indomitable against the weather as it had for eons.

"It does."

"Thought you'd fooled 'em all did ye?" Jethro crackled. "Thought ye'd waited long enough, didn't ye? You don't fool old Jethro Partridge, boy. I read ye plain."

He swung his gray away, still cackling, and Shelter felt a chill climb his spine which was not born of the rain. It was plain fear. The old man was happy now, madly so. But he was a killing thing, and when the time came, he would kill Shelter.

He worked at his ropes, trying to free a hand, knowing all the time that a free hand would do little to save Violet, to combat four rifles. He succeeded in rubbing raw grooves in his wrists, and gaining half an inch or so of slack. Rain washed the blood away; rain washed his hair into his eyes, soaked his shirt and jeans, beat against him like a drumming curse.

They wound along the halfway bluff. They saw no one else on the trail, although the signs of wagons were plentiful. Jethro had chosen this day because of the bad weather. There were no workers on the mountain. No one to stop them.

Workers—workers for what purpose? It nagged at Shelter's mind, but he kept drawing a blank. The dark men. The gold. The wagons. Benton Gray. All the elements in the equation. Totalled they still equalled zero.

Of course there was the final element—Lookout Mountain. The cedars at the base of the mountain were scorched black by warfires. The stone itself was burned. There were tunnels carved into its stony heart, places where men had been shot like fish in a barrel. Some, they said, had simply been sealed up. That was as effective as anything—with no prisoners to worry about.

The trees likely would never grow back. But Lookout had endured the war. It would endure.

It was a black and stormy hour when they achieved the summit. Below, the world was a frothing wash of rain and mottled cloud. Nothing green showed across all of the world. All was gray and cold, cold black. Jethro stepped down, rubbing his hands against the cold. Lavelle lifted Violet from her horse and then cut Shelter's ropes.

Shell slid to the stone, legs cramped, teeth chattering. There was a tunnel entrance before them. A dark eye peering out at the stormy world. Three wagons sat to one side. Tarps had been thrown over their contents.

"What's that?" Shell asked, nodding at the wagons.

"Puzzles ye, don't it?" Jethro laughed. "Have a look, boy. It don't matter now."

Shelter shrugged and moved through the rain and wind to the nearest wagon. The corner of the tarpaulin fluttered free as he untied the half-hitch in the line.

Lifting it he smiled darkly. He nodded his belated understanding and retied the tarp. Violet was watching as he strode back to where the Partridges, backs to the wind, waited.

"Wh-what?" she asked, her teeth chattering. "What is it?"

"Cannon. Cannon and balls. A few crates of rifles."

"You'd be surprised how much Bragg left behind when he took off into Georgia," Jethro said. "Not countin' the gold—thought maybe Gray would've found that too, but I guess

157

it's hid real good."

"Yes. But how can this be all worth his while?" Shelter asked.

"How?" Jethro echoed mockingly. "How could it not be? All Gray needed was the equipment and the right connections. I guess he made them through government channels somewheres. You ken how many cannon he's plucked off of Lookout? Two hundred, boy. Know how many rifles? I never counted 'em but they's been twenty wagonloads."

"Where is he selling them?"

"Where the next war is going to happen. The way I hear it things is hot between the Roosians and the Turks, and weapons is at a premium, Morgan. That Turkish Sultan, he sent his boys all the way over here—Europe's a closed market for them Turks, the way Gray tells it.

"The cannon is old, some rusty, some spiked. But the Turks don't give a damn. The Roosians got nothing better. Them rifles is musket loaders," Jethro winked. "Same story there—they's the best, even second-hand and rusted that them Turks have seen. And don't you think Gray's asking a pretty penny for this stuff!"

"It's all illegal as hell."

"Damn right," Jethro said in an indifferent tone. "So's makin' whiskey. Think the hill folks will ever stop?"

"Mebbe we will," Tom Partridge suggested. "Soon as we're rolling in gold."

"And that'll be soon, won't it Cousin Morgan?"

"Real soon. Though it's a tough spot to get to. Listen, why not let Violet go now? She can't foul this up now."

"I like havin' her near, boy," Jethro said. "Lavelle likes it too."

"All right." Shelter sent out a feeler, trying to gauge Jethro's mind. "Say we find the gold. What's my share?"

"What the hell you mean 'Say we find it,' you damn well *better* find it!"

"I will," Shelter said reassuringly. "As long as Gray hasn't buried it deeper, maybe shoving tailings down the wrong shaft right on top of that gold."

"Looky," Jethro said softly. "Say we find the gold — you get a fair share, boy. Say we *don't* ... " he shook his head. "You a dead man, son."

"We'll find it," Shelter said confidently, trying hard to paint a look of belief on his face. Did Jethro think him stupid enough to believe that the mountain man would let him live? Shelter hoped so just then. It might loosen things up just enough.

"Rain's comin' in," Lavelle said. "We're findin' nothin' standin' here jawin'."

"You're right," Jethro agreed. The wind whipped the rain across the stone ledge, lifting their coattails. "Let's get to it. Tom, gather up the lanterns. Lavelle, move into the tunnel ahead of Cousin Morgan."

They moved silently inside, the rain falling behind them. The wind was muffled to a whisper inside the dark honeycombed mountain. Lavelle's lantern swung at his side as he moved along a narrow corridor of stone, angling left at Shelter's instruction.

Now Shelter was in deep. He had no idea where they were, why Jethro was determined to believe this was the right area to search. He began to wonder if the old man was completely sane. The lanternlight danced in his eyes as they moved through the tunnel.

The more he turned that over in his mind, the more insane Jethro seemed. He had burned a witch at the stake, believing she had caused his stock to come down sick. He took as gospel the story that the gold lay hidden in his mountain. He had never bothered to ask Shelter where the gold was hidden. He was dead certain it was here, and he was fixated by the conclusion.

A sane man would consider many possibilities — the gold had been here, was never here, might be here — as Mason Plank had, coming to a negative conclusion. But not Jethro.

They ducked under a low ceiling of stone and at that moment the shocking suspicion came to Shelter — who would have murdered his father? What was it Jethro believed? The answer to that was that Jethro Partridge believed he had the right to kill whenever he wished it. Aaron Plank, the Witch Woman, his father . . . ?

It couldn't be. Why? He recalled then Mason Plank's words — *Who else we got so be-damned dirty and vicious in these hills?*

Who else indeed?

But Pa had been a member of the clan. *Like I am,* Shelter thought bitterly. He knew his father had never gone along with feuds and malicious mischief. Shelter studied Partridge with new understanding. He had no proof except for the suspicion which rode his guts poisonously, yet that was almost enough. Almost.

Water seeped down the cold stone as they angled left and downward, creeping into the cold maw of Lookout. Breath steamed from their lips, drifting before the lanterns. Shelter's feet and hands were stiff, his damp body was frozen. The lanterns glared on the rough granite walls, casting moving ghostly shadows.

Shelter was worried. Suppose they dead-ended at a place where there was obviously no gold? The honeycomb of man-cut and water-cut tunnels was vastly confusing. None of them knew where they were. But Shelter knew they would end up nowhere at all.

"How much farther?" Lavelle complained.

"Keep going," Shelter told him.

Jethro barked—"Stay a good distance out front, Lavelle! Don't want the boy taking off on us."

That was exactly what Shelter wanted. The chance to take off. Any sort of a chance. First he needed to have Violet next to him so that they could make their try together. Otherwise he would be dooming her. Secondly he needed a gun. He saw no chance for either possibility.

Lavelle had reached a sharp rise in the tunnel. A sort of step where a man had to clamber up six feet in order to continue.

The big man hesitated and Jethro shouted, "What's the matter with you! Get on up!" His voice echoed through the vast, empty chambers.

Lavelle spun around angrily, thought better of talking back and climbed up, first tossing up his rifle, setting his lantern on the ledge.

With a grunt he pulled himself up, got a leg on the ledge and rolled in, momentarily out of their sight. It gave Shelter an idea.

"Someone's going to have to help the girl up," he said.

"I'll do it," Bob Partridge offered, starting to put his rifle down.

"No, Bob." Jethro's eyes glittered with foxy intelligence. Was Cousin Morgan trying something? "You he'p her, Morgan."

"All right." He stretched out a hand to Violet, but Jethro slapped it away.

"Wait a minute! Lavelle!" he called. "Everything all right?"

"Yeah. It's just . . . it goes down sharp from here."

"Step back! The girl's comin' up. Then Morgan. Keep back and cock that rifle!"

The old man smiled wolfishly at Shelter. "Now," he said, waving his hand.

Shelter cupped his hands and Violet stepped into them. He raised high and saw her grapple and then skitter over the rim.

"Now you," Jethro said.

Shell looked up, nodded, and leaped up, grasping the cold rough stone.

Now! It had to be now. It was a slim chance, but there might never be another. Shelter pulled himself up and rolled onto the ledge.

He rolled and kept rolling. Lavelle was six feet away and Shelter sent his body tumbling into Lavelle's. The rifle in Lavelle's hands exploded with thunder, ear-shattering in the close confines, and the bullet slammed past Shelter's head, ricocheting wildly off down the tunnels, spraying Shell's face with granite slivers.

He took Lavelle at the knees and knocked him down before he could fire again. The big man's head slammed back against the stone and he lay there.

"Run!" Shelter hollered at Violet. *Run where?* If she had asked that, Shelter would have no answer for her, but she followed his order without hesitation, snatching up the lantern which mercifully had not broken.

Shell snatched up Lavelle's Spencer, saw a hand and rifle barrel appear over the ledge and ducked aside just as the muzzle flared up crimson and angry yellow. Shelter stomped down hard on the hand, saw the rifle fall free, heard an enraged roar, and then he was off and running, ducking low to clear the ceiling of rough stone.

Three shots followed rapidly, each bullet shattering into a dozen deadly fragments which crisscrossed the tunnel with frantic ricocheting lead.

He could no longer see the lantern ahead of him, but only those behind him. He crashed into a wall of stone painfully before he saw the elbow bend the tunnel made, and again saw the wavering lantern Violet held. She waited for him as he ran to her.

"Off," he told her. "Turn it off."

She did so, the lanternlight being swallowed up instantly by the cold darkness. Shelter dropped to prone and cocked Lavelle's rifle, his heart pounding.

He heard the rush of feet, saw a lantern and he fired, putting out the lamp. Now they were all in the darkness, and it evened things up.

Shelter backed away slowly, leading Violet. After a dozen steps he put another shot in the direction of the Partridges just to give them something to think about. The Spencer carried seven shots, that gave him five left and none to waste.

They moved by feel along the slightly upward angle of the passageway. Now and then Shelter stopped to listen, but he heard no following footsteps. He was not lulled into believing that Jethro Partridge had given up, however; and he had a sudden chilling thought that the old man somehow knew these passageways and might even know how to get ahead of them.

The idea was not so far-fetched. Jethro Partridge had lived near Lookout all his life, and between the end of the war and the time

Benton Gray had moved in and put up his fences, there had been plenty of time for exploration—especially by a man who thought there was gold up here.

He had Violet's hand in his; she led now, holding the dead lantern. They made a tight U-bend and started up more steeply.

Suddenly she was not there. She yanked hard at Shelter's hand and he just managed to keep his balance. He pulled her up and stood silently cursing, his face drenched with perspiration. There in the floor of the cave was an unseen verticle drop. The rocks and dust trickled away into the pit and it was a long, long time before they struck bottom.

"The lantern?" she asked. She clung to him, her heart racing.

"Yes," Shelter agreed reluctantly. They might not see the next shaft, and that would make the problem of Jethro Partridge academic. The lantern flared to life as Violet touched her wavering blue match flame to it. She turned it as low as possible in order to conserve the fuel and to cloak their visibility.

Still the lantern was astonishingly bright after the total darkness and as it caught and glowed in the stone corridor, Violet gasped, nearly dropping the lantern.

"Hello, boys," Shelter said.

They were there still. Guns in bony fingers. Learning against the walls helter-skelter, jumbled together in vanished emotions. Men still fighting the long-ago war. Skeletons in rotten bits of uniforms, gray and blue tangled together in frozen violence.

The lanternlight caught a bit of silver, the ivory of the bones, the rusted barrel of a gun. A detached, hollow-eyed skull peered up at them and a rat darted for the darkness, out of the grinning skull's mouth.

"You did your best, men," Shelter said softly. His voice was respectful and it shocked Violet to hear him speaking to them as if they still lived. Then she realized that there was every chance that Shelter could have known some of them; she realized as he did that he could very easily be lying there among them, silent, cold in the damp tomb.

They picked their way through the scattered bones, careful to disturb nothing. Then they moved on, more quickly.

They walked until exhaustion clung to them like their damp clothing, until the light in the lamp began to flicker and dim as the fuel expired. They traced a maze, passing the same point three or four times in their dizzy confusion. The tunnels climbed, fell, turned left and then right without pattern, spraying off through the intestines of the mountain.

"If the lamp goes out," Violet panted, "we'll never . . . "

"Shut up!" Shelter said sharply. "Just move."

"All right." Violet nodded wearily, and her eyes, unnaturally bright in the lanternlight, met Shell's. Then she smiled. "All right."

They found an upward pointing trail, and

dead-ended. Backing out they found another fork. The ceiling was low, but they elected to try it. A hundred feet and the lantern went out and they were frozen, immobile in the darkness.

"Oh, God, Shelter!" A vivid image flashed through Violet's mind. Two skeletons wound together in this narrow, cold chamber. Two more victims of Lookout Mountain.

"Keep moving," Shelter said.

"I . . . can't."

"Do it!"

He put a hand on her rump and shoved her ahead of him. They crawled on, the ceiling lowering, the stone scraping their kneecaps, their hands. Water sheeted past beneath them. Each breath, each movement, was echoed through the chamber. Violet's heartbeat drummed in her ears.

She moved through a blur of reality. Dark stone, cold, a man pushing her forward when she wanted to stop, to sleep, to die perhaps.

She fought her way along, legs and arms cramping. Was there no end to the climbing? Her head swam, she saw color, light where there was none. The lantern in her hand seemed to sparkle, briefly, to flare up and she laughed at herself.

"What is it?" Shelter wanted to know.

"I thought . . . " she giggled hysterically. And then it did it again. The lantern somehow brought back to life. She saw the wink of pure, white light in the glass. "The lantern," she explained, holding it up.

Shelter sighed and lifted his weary eyes. It couldn't . . .

Yes, the lantern *was* lit, by God!

The lantern, hell! He rushed forward. It was not lanternlight at all but a single, faint beam of sunlight striking the chimney of the lantern. There! A tiny keyhole through the stone wall surrounding them. Shelter clawed at it, found that it was turf and not stone and dug faster, ripping sod free until the gray light of day winked at them, and then the hole was large enough.

Shelter wriggled through, helped Violey up and they stood unsteadily. The wind washed over them, a spattering of raindrops. The land was gray, stormy around them. And they walked to the edge of the earth, standing on the rim of Lookout Mountain, breathing in deep gasps of sweet, cold air.

"Glad you could join us, Cousin Morgan. Why don't ye just drop that rifle before I blow you plumb off the mountain."

Jethro Partridge was grinning savagely as Shelter turned to face him.

10.

The old man had lost his hat somewhere and his gray hair washed into his sullen eyes. His jaw worked restlessly as if he were chewing something or searching with his tongue for a word.

It was neither. It was the uncontrolled spasms of a man not quite in control of himself. Shelter knew now that his guesswork about Jethro had been largely accurate — the man was out of touch with reason.

"They's more than one way up here," Jethro said. He nodded vaguely and Shelter looked to the edge of the mountain. A trail no more than eighteen inches wide sloped sharply down away, disappearing as it made a bend behind a protruding bluish boulder and a weather-stunted cedar.

"I knew you'd be here. You had to come out, didn't ye?" Jethro mocked. His words were slurred now, even more than usual. His eyes were glitter bright. "I left the boys to watch below, but I knowed you'd climb, Cousin Morgan."

"Did you?" Shelter watched as the old man circled them slowly, his cocked rifle thrust out before him. Shelter knew they would die there, on this cold mountain top. Possibly Jethro would simply tumble them back into the hole, leaving it to Lookout to swallow the evidence of crime. "We can talk it over, Jethro," Shell suggested.

"The hell we can!" he shouted back through the rain. "Think I want that gold now! Tainted, it would be," he said nonsensically.

"Tainted?" Shell said mildly. He took a measuring step forward, but Jethro jabbed the rifle muzzle at him.

"Get back! Yeees," he drawled. "Tainted. I've been ponderin' that. It's Morgan gold. Dirty. You're like your Daddy, a traitor to the clan, traitors to the hill ways."

"So you'll kill me as you killed him."

"That's right!" Jethro snapped. "Oh, your

Pa was a sneaky one. Shinin' up to me one minute, betrayin' me the next. A coward, a shame to the clan."

"How did you do it?" Shelter asked. His mind was twisting and tumbling, trying to find a way out of this.

"Sly, boy! I did him sly. *He* didn't even know it was me that done it. He was having a whiskey, back to me and I gave it to him. Baling wire, Cousin Morgan. I used baling wire, sharpened like a needle. I come behind him and give it to him under the eighth rib, driving it to his heart. He made a little gurgling sound and bent against the bar. I pulled it free and cozied to him. 'What's the matter, Morgan?' I asked him and he slapped at his back. 'Little pain,' he says."

"You punctured his heart."

"That's right. With no more pain than a case of indigestion. Then. Later the blood seeps out and a man feels the trickling, wondering what it is. I've stuck many a pig that way, boy. The bleeding keeps the meat fresh."

A sickness rolled up in Shelter's belly. The ugly glee in Jethro's eyes sickened him beyond nausea. This dirty, withered man had killed his father. A good father he had been, a kind man, twice Jethro's worth. Shelter felt his throat constrict, felt his stomach tighten, his fists ball up.

He wanted to lunge at Jethro Partridge, tear his throat from his living body and hurl him from Lookout Mountain. He fought it back,

171

knowing that was suicide for both him and Violet.

Jethro sighted down his rifle barrel and Shelter heard Violet gasp in terror. Looking into those eyes now, Shelter saw the same sort of careless malice, the same inhuman tolerance for brutality he had seen in Lavelle's eyes, and he wondered why he had not been sharp enough to notice that before — it might have saved his life.

"So long, Cousin Morgan," Jethro said, his voice rolling with dark amusement. Shelter bunched his muscles, ready to try one last desperate leap. He watched Jethro's dark eyes sparkle savagely.

And then the eyes changed. Uneasiness crept in. Fear and then stark terror. The blood washed out of his face and his arms trembled. He backed away, lowering the rifle.

"No," he murmured. "No!" His eyes were horror-struck, and then from the tail of his eye Shelter saw her.

Witch Woman. She wore black. A veil hung over her head, her dress was trailing against the damp earth. Knobby, bare feet tracked forward slowly, steadily, unalterable and evenly cadenced as a pendulum.

Jethro backed away, his rifle now loose in his hand, old tales of terror, disbelief, frantic fear working together in his mind.

"You're dead!" he screamed.

Her voice was cracked, strained, deep baritone. "Can't be killed," she intoned as she

172

continued her inexorable march toward the mountain man who cowered at the edge of the mountain, a forearm up to shield his face.

"I burnt ye! You dead!"

"Can't be killed," she repeated tonelessly. Then, amazingly, she cackled, a screech of delicious joy, and she threw back the veil which covered her face.

"Dear God," Violet moaned.

Her face was a skull, hairless, burned to a permanently blistered dreadfulness. Her lips had been peeled back by torture. She had no eyebrows, no lashes, no hair on her head. She laughed again and drew nearer to Jethro who trembled violently, his heart pounding against his ribcage as if begging to be released so it could flee this witch, this death, this thing.

"Oh, Sweet Jesus!" Jethro murmured, dropping his rifle.

"He cain't hear you, Jethro Partridge. Pray to your maker — pray to your great god, Lucifer! You'll see him now, you'll suffer the flames. The painful, flesh devouring flames. The unspeakable pain, the sound of your own meat crackling in your ears. Now!"

She lurched forward, tripping over a stone, and Jethro leaped back. His foot slipped and his arms flailed wildly. They had a last vision of him, eyes wide, mouth open in soundless screaming before he toppled over the rim of the mountain and was gone, cartwheeling through silent space.

Violet clung to Shelter. The Witch Woman stood motionlessly on the edge of the mountain, the wind washing over her, twisting her black garments. Then she lowered her veil and turned, coming back to them.

"There's a way down. Follow me," she said.

Shelter picked up Jethro's rifle, glancing once down at the gray, cloud clotted emptiness. He turned and led Violet, following the old woman, who was light on her feet, silent as a dark ghost. They slipped into a tunnel partly concealed by brush and boulders and wove into a larger passageway. It was dark, but Shelter could see torches fixed into the passageway walls. Ahead a faint glimmer of firelight showed and they rounded a bend into a chamber cluttered with the odd and the bizarre.

Dead bats in a fruit jar, hooves cut from deer and from cattle, weirdly sketched pictures of bizarre, wide-eyed demons on the smoky walls, a flat, straw stuffed mattress, a huge black kettle, a bundle of rags, a burlap sack which contained something round and the size of a human head . . . Violet trembled in his arms.

They waited, unmoving, only their breathing stirring the silence as the Witch Woman gathered a few things in a gunny sack.

"Prob'ly won't be safe here no more," she muttered, snatching up items—bags of herbs: wolfbane, hemlock, yarrow dust.

She turned to face them, her mummy's skull faintly outlined behind the veil. "All right. We'll get along."

174

"Are you going to tell me about it?" Shelter asked.

"As we walk," she said with reluctance.

Witch Woman hefted a torch, struck flint and turned it as it glowed up hotly. She touched the fire to the belongings she left behind and nodded.

They followed her into a tunnel which opened onto a mammoth cavern. A steep, water-slick path led down into the blue, yawning maw. Stalactites and stalagmites blossomed from the stone like cold sabers. Water dripped off somewhere, and beyond that Shelter heard the sound of rushing, bubbling water as an underground river gurgled past.

The torchlight cast long, crooked shadows against the water polished walls of the cavern. She began to speak.

"It was 'cause of me your Daddy was killed. He knew Jethro's plan to kill me. Your Daddy said it was madness. Said I couldn't have sickened his cows. Then Jethro . . . did that thing to me."

"They all thought you were dead," Shelter said. They stepped cautiously across a sulphurous smelling stream and began climbing a chute on the far side.

"Dead. Was I? I don't even know. Maybe my heart stopped — it had good cause. Someone took me down. It was cold, snowing, but I couldn't feel the cold nor any pain. My nerve endings had been melted off. The men were going to bury me, but it was cold and they left me.

"When they come back," she said. "I was gone. Folks figured wolves got me. But I was still alive. I crawled. I crawled and it was snowing. My flesh peeled off me and I crawled on and I hid, waiting to die, wanting to die. But I didn't. Lord let me live to do one deed for him."

"Jethro, you mean."

"Yes. I loved your Momma, your Daddy. Only folks ever treated me like I was human. Broke my heart when your Ma died. Then I had to watch you bury your Daddy, Shelter. I came to the burying if you recall. I ran away when you saw me. I can imagine what you'd of thought of my face ... and then you left. I was alone and I cured myself with herbs. Healed as well as a body in that condition could heal.

"And I began to wait, to watch. I prowled Jethro Partridge's farm, watching and waiting. But I was sceered and there was never the chance. Then I saw you had come back, Shelter and my heart worried over you—I knew he'd kill you. Knew it."

"But for you, he would have." Shelter answered. "I can't thank you enough."

"No. It was my way of thankin' your Daddy." They burst suddenly into the rain washed freshness of clear air and Witch Woman said, "This is all I can do. Get now."

"I'll be back to visit," Shelter promised. "If you'll tell me where ... "

"Go. Don't come back!" she said sternly. "I

want to see no more human men, Shelter. Including you. No more! I'll be in the woods or in the wind," she said, her voice trailing off. "In the rain . . ." and she turned, walking away from them, her arms crossed, her back straight, a diminishing, tragic figure in black, vanishing into the rain.

They watched her a moment, and then a moment longer until finally she was gone. Once they heard a weird shriek fill the day, but they convinced themselves it was the wind in the cave.

"Now what?" Violet asked. The rain soaked through her shirt, her dark hair hung limply. Shelter put a hand on her head, drawing her near for his kiss.

"Now we live."

He felt her arms go around him, felt her give way to the tears which had been building all day and he held her tightly, petting her hair.

"How do we get out of here, Violet?" Shelter asked. "Bob and Tom are out there somewhere, watching the roads. Lavelle. Gray's men, I suppose."

She was thoughtful, then her face brightened. "If it weren't raining . . ." the light in her eyes dimmed out. Shelter prodded her,

"If it weren't raining, what?"

"I used to come up here with Aaron. Years back. We'd raft on down the creek. It flows right past our place, you know. But in this rain . . ."

"It's a chance. Better than we've got on the roads."

"But we had a raft . . . it may still be there!"

"Show me."

They spent most of an hour looking. Violet became confused and then desperate. Finally they did find what remained of the raft, hidden under an overgrowth of vines and scrub oak. They dragged it out onto the riverbank, and Shelter got to work, binding the old, rotten logs with his torn-up shirt and the few vines which were strong enough. It was a jerry-built, almost childlish appearing job when done.

"Maybe it's enough to get us downstream," he said dubiously.

"I guess it had better be," Violet said, and his eyes met hers in silent agreement. It was the only chance.

The water, swelled with raging runoff, rumbled past through the trees, and Shelter knew it had never been like that when Violet and her brother had taken their lazy summer journeys.

"Ready?" He held the raft, straining against the force of the rampaging water and Violet took a sharp breath and nodded, clambering aboard the pitching raft, clinging to it.

Shelter released the line and rolled aboard beside her. They lay side by side, clasping the outside logs and each other as the raging stream snatched at the rough raft and swept them downstream.

They ran swiftly but smoothly at first. Until they hit a creek ford where cobblestones had been dumped for a road bed. There the creek twisted and foamed up, throwing frothing spurs of water into the air. They skidded across the cobblestones, being turned and jolted. Shelter's knuckles were torn open by the stones as the bottom of the raft collided with the rocky bottom.

Free of that menace they paddled desperately, trying to turn the raft. But it turned of its own accord, spiralling down the rapids, past undercut trees and bobbing, treacherous sawyers.

"Look out!" Shelter had time to yell just before they collided with a rolling mass of tree roots. They crashed into it, their teeth jarred by the impact, spun away and continued on.

The river was clearer now, the elms and willows on either side arcing over them, shaking and trembling in the wind-driven rain.

The river widened, deepened and straightened. But its velocity only increased and they were hurtling down nature's millrace, clinging to the raft which had a tendency to heel over to the left corner and ride high, narrowly avoiding going over.

And then it did go and Shelter was thrown into the icy water, the corner of the raft ripping past his head, missing by scant inches. He swam with all his might, clutching at the raft, looking around frantically for Violet who was lost in the white water which frothed up all around them.

His stroking hand touched hair and he yanked at it, drawing her head briefly above the water. Her mouth opened for air and the foam swelled over her.

Clinging to the raft with one hand, to Violet with the other, Shelter's body was twisted and battered by the locomotive force of the raging river. He had been in high surf which was less torrential; the river seemed determined to claim them.

Shelter gave a desperate tug on Violet's hair, feeling the raft's rough wood slip inexorably from his grasp. Then, somehow, she was up. clinging to his neck and with her free hand she grasped the raft and dragged herself onto what had been, moments ago, the bottom side of it.

They narrowly missed a giant stream bed boulder, and skirted a stand of live oaks growing out of the river bed, only their tops showing above the deep current.

Then it seemed they had passed the worst of it. The river roared on, muddied, frothing through what had to be Benton Gray's land. Craning his neck, Shelter could see the retreating bulk of Lookout and he called:

"Almost made it now!"

"Almost!" Violet found a weak smile and put it on for Shell. She coughed violently three times, spitting up water.

At last they reached the grasslands and the water spread out, the river slowing as it rolled on, meandering now, forking into two creeks.

They could talk now without shouting above the roar of the river and Violet told him, "When I used to do this with Aaron, I always thought how fine it would be to float down a lazy river with a man who wasn't my brother. I couldn't have imagined *that*," she added with a shudder.

"One day we'll do it, Violet. On a lazy day." He smiled and she returned his smile. Her hand rested on his back and she gave him a squeeze.

The river returned to the forests; dark shadows blotted out the sun as the rain came down. Shelter was shivering as he had been shivering all day. It seemed there had never been a time when he was not wet, cold, battered and miserable. But he held on, knowing as Violet did that they were nearly safe. It couldn't be another mile to the Plank farm and warmth, shelter and food.

At last they rounded the big bend in the river and ahead Violet saw the corner of the roof which was her father's house. She lifted a finger and Shelter nodded.

Getting off the raft proved to be as tricky as getting on it. They eventually plunged into the water, letting the raft spin on downstream as they swam against the furious current toward the bank. Shelter grabbed a tree root and held on until Violet caught his leg and then they moved up, rising shakily to the muddy bank.

The house was several hundred yards off— they had overshot it by that much, but they walked arm in arm through the downpour, their spirits high. Smoke rose from the chimney of the house, promising warmth and comfort. They could smell beans cooking and they increased their pace.

They rounded the corner of the farmhouse and came face to face with the lawman. His badge glinted on his heavy macintosh and in his hands was a non-nonsense double-ten express gun. Other men drifted in from out of the trees.

"Shelter Morgan? I'm Sheriff Dantley. We've some talking to do, boy."

11.

Sheriff Dantley had alert green eyes flanking a slightly ambitious nose. His skin had been tanned to leather by sun and wind, and the lines around the eyes had been deeply engraved. He was the sort of man Shelter did not want to argue with—at least not while he held that shotgun, and Shelter nodded.

"All right. Let's talk."

"Inside," Dantley said. He stepped back as Shelter went past him and through the doorway. Mason Plank was there and a second lawman. A tall, lanky man with a drooping mustache and a United States marshal's badge pinned to a loose white shirt.

"This him?" the marshal asked, standing. Dantley nodded. Violet Plank rushed past to embrace her father. The old man was concerned, obviously.

"Sit down, Morgan," the sheriff said. "This is Marshal Ken Johnson."

Shelter took a seat and he glanced up to take a cup of coffee from Dantley. The sheriff squared a chair around to face Morgan, but it was the marshal who spoke.

"I finally get to meet you," Johnson said. Shelter frowned at him, not getting it. The marshal explained, "I'm down from Washington, Morgan. You're not entirely unknown to us. You've gotten around a good deal of country and raised a deal of hell."

"Not unnecessarily, and not criminally," Shelter said.

"There's a dead Turkish national in Whynot," the Marshal went on.

"Is there?" Shelter sipped his coffee.

"Yes." The marshal paced the floor. "That's a matter which could have international repercussions."

"I would suppose it could," Shelter agreed.

"Did you do it?"

"Someone says I did? A witness, maybe?"

"Not exactly."

"I suppose," Shelter said quietly, "if I had

done such a thing there would have been a reason for it. If I had done it, it would only be because two Turkish nationals jumped me in the alleyway and tried to cut off some of the necessary parts of my anatomy."

"If you had done it," Dantley put in.

"Correct."

"You're cool, Morgan," Johnson chuckled. "They told me you were."

"Did they?"

"Yes, like I say, you're not unknown to us. There's a report on my desk of an interview some time back with an assistant Secretary of War. You came out and told him what you intended to do."

"Did I? I can't recall. A man gets wild notions sometimes. Sometimes it takes a while to cool down." Shelter put his empty cup aside.

"When you think you might cool down, Morgan?" Ken Johnson asked, his expression unreadable.

"Soon," Morgan said, shooting him a flat smile.

"You know Elizabeth Townshend?" he asked out of the blue. Shelter knew his face responded to that. He felt a hot flush creep across his face. Violet glanced questioningly at him.

"I know her," he replied.

"I know you do. She turned in a very interesting report after she returned from Mexico. As I say, you have a reputation in Washington . . . for several reasons."

"Look," Shelter flared up, "if you've come here to badger me ..."

"I haven't," Johnson answered quickly. "I just wanted to have a little talk. We're here for something else entirely. We're going after Benton Gray, Morgan. I figured you might want to be in on it."

"Gray!"

"That's right. You're not the only one who got suspicious. Sheriff Dantley here has been poking around judiciously for quite a while. The United States government, as you might suppose frowns on state senators war-profiteering with government material. We were on our way out there when word came from Mister Plank that his daughter was missing, and was in the company of a Mister Shelter Morgan. It wasn't hard to figure what was up—what was difficult was figuring how you hoped to get out of there alive."

"You wouldn't believe how we did get back."

"No," Johnson looked at Shell and shook his head, "from what I've heard of you, I probably wouldn't. We're riding in an hour, Morgan. If you want to go along, arm yourself and get some dry clothing. I'll make it legal," he said, "as a matter of fact I guess you can have your choice of being a deputy marshal or a deputy sheriff."

"Whichever's quickest, Johnson," Shelter answered. He had peeled off his shirt and was towelling off with the towel Alexander

186

had handed him. "Because I was lying to you. I don't expect to cool off real soon. Not as long as Benton Gray is alive and free."

"I don't expect him to be both when the day's over," the marshal said dryly. "Have something to eat. I've got to brief my men. Mister Plank? If you'd be kind enough to describe the layout of the Gray place again to my deputies?"

Plank nodded and got up, going out to the barn where the task force waited. Shelter slipped into some of Alexander's clothing and gulped two cups of coffee with Violet's nervous eyes on him.

"You don't have to go. They'll get him now."

"I want to see it. I want him to see me," Shelter said.

"I don't want you to die."

"I'll be back. We've a trip to take together, remember?" He kissed her forehead and smiled. Then Shelter turned sharply, pulling on Mason Plank's old raincoat. They weren't leaving for an hour, but Shelter wanted to be in on the briefing. He wanted to riding *now*. And by sundown he wanted to see Benton Gray's hide tacked to a barn door.

The men, all in yellow slickers, were gathered in the barn A few heads turned when Shelter came in and Marshal Johnson called Shell to the front of the crowd.

"Boys," Johnson said, "this is Shelter Morgan. I wanted you to have a good look at him.

187

We don't want anybody shooting our own men."

Shelter nodded and stepped aside. The others were all in the same yellow raincoats for identification in case things got confused.

Looking around, Shelter recognized a handful of them. Mostly they were Johnson's deputies, or those of Dantley with a few volunteer hill country men sprinkled in.

"Mister Plank will go over the layout of the countryside once more, listen up!" Johnson called.

Mason Plank talked then, in his slow drawling voice, pausing to scratch a map on the barn wall. When he was through Johnson got up again and tacked a plan for Gray's house up, pointing out every man's route. He had taken the time to get it from Benton Gray's architect, and Shell decided that Marshal Ken Johnson was a very thorough man.

"Morgan," he said, "you'll side me through the front door, assuming we get that far. Boys, you'll give every Gray man a chance to surrender, but not at the risk of your own lives. Some of those men, remember, are likely to be married men trying to pick up a few dollars riding fence . . . others," he also reminded them, "are likely to be the hardest cases you'll ever come across. Play it fair, but watch your own hides. Good luck."

They saddled in the deep shadows beneath the trees and rode out in a loose column through the stormy day. The sun was fading fast above the western mountains, the wind rising, pushing leaves across their path. Violet Plank stood in the doorway, a shawl around her, arms crossed beneath her breasts.

Shelter lifted his hand to her once and then turned and never looked back.

It would be full dark when they hit Gray's ranch. That was the way Johnson had wanted it, and it was probably safest, but Shelter had learned a long while ago, that it's easier by far to fight what you can see. In the darkness every tree seems to have a sniper behind it, and the shadowy man rushing toward you may be friend or enemy—it freezes a man, makes him hesitant, and in battle the hesitant man is the dead one.

They splashed across the creek, the horses throwing up silver spurs of water, and entered the dark oak forest to the east. Shelter remembered this area, but not well.

He rode close to Johnson in the darkness. The men were nervous—from time to time you could hear a man cock his weapon, wanting to be ready. It was hazardous and a little foolish, but Johnson didn't want to speak to warn them.

They rode through the oaks, water dripping from the trees, the only sounds the creaking of leather, the whispering of the horses' hoofs against the mulch and mud underfoot.

They came upon it suddenly. At least three lights were on in the dark bulk of Benton Gray's big house. Johnson held his rifle high in the air, bringing the column to a halt as they studied the house. The front door opened and by that light they could make out two armed guards on the broad, stone-walled veranda.

The wind was in Shelter's face, lifting his horse's mane. The rain had slackened and here and there a cold star could be made out, glimmering through the broken clouds.

"All right," Johnson whispered. He waved his hand and at the signal his men spread out, filtering through the shadows. It would take the best part of an hour for the force which was to enter from the rear to achieve their position.

There would be no signal from those men to show they were ready. Johnson would simply assume they had made it if they heard no gunfire. Shelter stepped out of leather and squatted on the earth, holding his horses' reins. Ken Johnson squinted at his pocket watch, grunted and stepped down as well, the horse shifting its feet.

A light went out in the house, another lantern was lit in a room farther back. They heard nothing but the clattering of the wind in the tree leaves. Once Shelter saw a pair of men on horseback leave the house and angle toward the west. He glanced at Johnson. There was every chance those riders would intercept the deputies, but there was no hope for it.

All they could do was wait. Wait until the hour had dragged past or until the first bark of a rifle signalled the beginning of the battle.

Shelter's horse bowed its neck and nuzzled him with a cold, wet nose. A tree behind the party dropped a branch to the wind, the cracking of the limb startlingly loud, startlingly like a gunshot and Shelter saw men's heads jerk around, hands tense involuntarily.

Shelter was a patient waiter. He had waited for battle before this. Long, cold waits for orders from distant command posts during which the muscles cramped, the eyes grew bleary from the watching, the nerves raw and ragged with the expected violence. He was a good waiter, but he didn't like it any better than the others. He knew what their thoughts were for they were the same as his ... let's get on with it. Win or lose, live or die. We've come for a fight, let's have at it.

It is an oddly prevalent reaction in a species which is so seemingly devoted to self-preservation. Perhaps it is simply that the nerves can only take so much.

"Let's go," Johnson whispered and Shell rose, mounting. He had his rifle in hand, his slicker drawn back for access to the Colt. He took his hat off and rolled it, putting it in his saddlebags, figuring to lose it anyway.

The men crowded close to Johnson, their horses dancing impatiently and then the marshal moved out, Sheriff Dantley and Shelter flanking him.

They walked the horses across the star-glossed grass, creeping nearer, expecting the first shot at any moment. Shelter's ears rang, his mouth was dry. He kept his eyes fixed on the two guards they could see.

One of the guards suddenly jumped, shouted out and the muzzle flash, red against the night, preceded a bullet which sang past overhead.

They started their horses to running. There was no command from Johnson, no need for one.

The two guards crouched behind the low wall and fired rapidly. Beside Shelter a horse shrieked its pain and a man was thrown free.

Shell's rifle was in his hands and he rode at a charge, reins looped around the pommel, his hands free to work the rifle. He levered through four shots. Everyone was firing. The stone wall of the veranda sang with ricochets; powdered stone puffed into the air and the two guards sagged back.

One of them was hit, the second tried for the door of the house. Finding it locked behind him he swung to make his fight.

He was too slow. Dantley, leaping his horse onto the veranda, shoved his pistol nearly against the man's chest and touched off. The guard was slammed back against the wall, his rifle clattering free.

Shelter dismounted at a run, achieved the wall and ducked low to evade a shot from the near window. Shell lifted up, fired through the glass, seeing the curtains jump with the impact of bullets, and leaped the wall, reaching the door at the same time Johnson did.

The marshal looked at Shelter, nodded, and Shell put his foot to the door. It took three tries but the door sprang open and Johnson made his rush, Shelter behind him. There were three men in the room which was a sort of vestibule with a high ceiling and tile floor. They had apparently been playing cards. A table was tipped over for a shield and cards lay everywhere.

The guards opened up with a hail of gunfire as the two men smashed into the room. A man just behind Shell groaned with pain as a bullet punched into his chest. Johnson took a man with his handgun and then the marshal was spun around, hit by a bullet through his arm. Shelter dove at the table, firing as he dove. One of the guards, raising up at the wrong instant, was killed by Shelter's bullet through his throat.

Another man behind the table was already dead. A third tried to crawl away on useless legs, blood smearing the floor beneath him. Shelter turned back toward the marshal.

Johnson was wounded seriously, pain engraved on his face, but he waved an angry hand, urging Shelter on. A yellow-clad deputy had slipped up beside Shelter, one of the few men Shelter knew, a hill boy named Walter Crabtree.

"Let's go," Shell said. The kid nodded, looking a little green around the gills. They crept forward, down the long corridor which led to Gray's office, hearing steady gunfire from outside the house on all sides.

They passed a lamp and Shell reached out to turn it out. Cautiously they moved past the doors facing the corridor, opening each in turn, Shelter's heart catching just a little at each try. The first three were empty, but in the fourth they came face to face with a balding, dark faced man in a silk nightshirt.

He sprang to his feet, shouting, "No shoot! No shoot!"

Shell nodded at the Turk telling Crabtree, "Take him in, but not too rough."

"Come along," Crabtree said, obviously not unhappy to be going the other way. He took the Turk in tow and walked back down the hall.

Shelter moved ahead. He found an empty kitchen, dishes spilled on the floor as men had taken off. A face appeared suddenly at a window, and Shelter was able to hold back. It was a deputy and his face washed white as he saw the big Colt in Shelter Morgan's hand thrust at him. He grinned finally, a sickly expression of relief, waved a hand and ducked away as Shelter crept on through the house.

The gunfire outside was more sporadic now. He heard Dantley's voice shouting something. Then Shelter was there.

The door was the entrance to Gray's office as they knew from the plan of the house. Shelter pressed himself against the wall and tried the knob. Instant gunfire answered the rattling of the knob.

Five bullets ripped through the meat of the

194

mahogany door, splintering the fancy carving on it. Shell took a deep breath, stepped out and fired two shots of his own, then he shouldered the door, rolling into the room to come up in a crouch.

A bullet whooshed past his ear, thudding into the plaster of the wall behind him and Shelter answered with his own shots. Two bullets, both on target, slammed into the body of the man behind the desk. He staggered back, his arms waving like windmills, his face a mask of blood.

Shelter leaped to the side and then stepped around the desk, his finger on the trigger of the big blue Colt. The man was dead, stretched out against the floor, a dark stain leaking out against the polished wood. Slowly Shelter rolled him over. Then he straightened up, just looking.

He heard footsteps in the corridor behind him and turned to see Dantley and a deputy rush in. Dantley slowed and strode across the room, holstering his gun. He stopped and looked at Shelter.

The deputy, an impatient red-faced kid asked excitedly, "Is that him? Is that Benton Gray sure enough?"

Shelter glanced at Dantley and answered in a soft voice, "No. No it's not, kid."

The man was a stranger to them. A full-bearded ox of a man, his face shattered by Shelter's bullet.

"How's Johnson?" Shell asked.

"He'll make it. We've got twelve prisoners.

Six guards dead. Three deputies won't make it back."

Shelter was silent, thoughtful. He stood limply, gun dangling in his hand and Dantley, reading his thoughts, said, "We've got this place surrounded, Morgan. There's no way in hell Benton Gray can escape."

"No," Shelter agreed. But already he had a sinking feeling in his guts. He knew already that the man was gone, and he stood there, looking at the dead man on the floor, the man who should have been Benton Gray.

12.

Marshal Ken Johnson was sagged in a velvet chair, his shirt sleeve slashed open, a hasty bandage being applied to his wound. He glanced up at Dantley and Shelter. Dantley just shook his head.

"The Turk is talking his head off. Claims he didn't know that any of this was illegal. He was dealing with a man in high office ... all crap, but he'll go on claiming innocence. We could never hold him anyway. I suppose he'll be travelling somewhere else looking to buy more weapons as soon as we've gotten his visa revoked."

He noticed the glum look on Shelter's face, and said, "Don't worry about Gray. Come dawn we'll fan out and find the good senator."

"We both know he could be a hundred miles away come sunup," Shell answered.

"Yes, he could be," Johnson nodded. "Look at it this way, Morgan. The man has lost his position, lost his house, lost his fortune. Maybe that's enough revenge."

"No," Shelter answered, his cold blue eyes meeting those of the marshal, "it isn't enough, Johnson. Not for me."

Morning was long in coming. They had found a wagon in the shed and the wounded were transported back to Whynot. Dantley, Shelter, and the remaining deputies spread out, circling the ranch, hoping to find some trace of Benton Gray, but with last night's rain, it seemed unlikely they'd find anything. The day was clear until mid-morning and then clouded up again. Shelter met Dantley at noon and the two men discussed it.

"Looks like he's slithered away," the sheriff said, mopping his forehead with a blue scarf. "But I can promise you he won't get out of my county, Shelter. I want him almost as badly as you do. I've got men on all the roads. Unless he can fly, we'll bring him in eventually."

They worked the area all afternoon, until

with daylight fading they had to give it up and return to the Gray house where they camped.

Shelter sat inside the circle of firelight, drinking coffee with the men. He had been gnawing at the problem, turning it this way and that.

Gray was gone. Not far. The roads, as Dantley promised, were all being watched, and Shell didn't make Gray for enough of a ridge-runner to make it cross-country. Where was he? How would Gray's thinking go?

He tried putting himself in Benton Gray's position. On the run, knowing the county was hemmed in. Try to break out? Or stay low, waiting until they gave up. Even if it took a month or two. Dantley couldn't hold his roadblocks indefinitely. Several of the deputies were already grousing about wanting to go home if the fighting was over.

All right—hole up, then. But a man would need supplies, and again Shelter didn't make Gray as being a man who could live off the land. What then? Sneak into Pikeville or raid the larder at a local farm? Risky business.

Unless he didn't have to worry about supplies!

Maybe a cautious man like Gray would have provided against a day like this. He was cunning enough, careful enough. All right, he had a hideout, a cache of food and ammunition . . . where?

Shelter's head turned slowly. He saw it through the veil of clouds, glinting in the starlight. Lookout Mountain stood bulky and mysterious against the evening sky, casting deep shadows across the land, and Shelter Morgan smiled.

It was a deep, warm smile. He knew. He knew where Gray would have planted his cache, where he would hide. Was there any place better?

He had a view of the surrounding country, a labyrinth to hide in. He obviously knew all of those tunnels by now. Probably he had stumbled across a perfect hideout. A hidden tunnel, a secret cavern. After all, even knowing a man was in there, it was unlikely he could be found. The smile on Shelter's face remained. He was certain, absolutely certain.

"I've got you, you son of a bitch," Shelter said under his breath. Dantley peered at him from across the flickering fire, his face questioning.

"Did you say something, Morgan?"

"No," Shell said, throwing the dregs of his coffee into the fire. He rose, stretching his arms, "Nothing at all. Believe I'll turn in, Sheriff." He walked away from the fire whistling and Dantley's eyes narrowed at the sight of a man who had worn a stone face all day suddenly acting cheerful as a mockingbird in a caterpillar tree. The sheriff watched Shelter until he blended with the shadows and became invisible against the darkness. Then Dantley shrugged and poured himself another cup of coffee.

Over the morning campfire Dantley suggested, "How about you and me taking a turn around the western boundary, we can check the three roadblocks over that way, then cut back and poke the brush along Miller's Run?"

"No, thanks," Shelter said over his coffee. "Thought I'd run into Pikeville and get a few things. Maybe check the hills over that way on the way back."

"Suit yourself," Dantley shrugged.

Shelter spent an hour after breakfast cleaning his weapons, stuffing the leftover biscuits into his saddlebags and graining the borrowed bay he rode. Dantley noticed it all but said nothing.

When Shelter did ride out it had begun to drizzle. He rode, a solitary figure, through the oaks and into the swirl of clouds and rain.

Crabtree came up beside Sheriff Dantley who was watching Shelter, hands on hips.

"Damn," the kid muttered, "I wanted to catch Morgan before he left. I could've used a few things from Pikeville myself."

"It would have been a long wait, Crabtree," Dantley said. The kid looked at Dantley curiously, but the sheriff turned away, striding toward his horse. He stopped and turned back. "Like to take a little ride around the western perimeter? It's a nice day for a ride."

Crabtree shook his head, not understanding the tone of indifference in the sheriff's voice. Searching for a wanted man was something Dantley never referred to so lightly. It was almost as if Dantley had decided that Gray was gone and there was no chance at all of finding him over west.

Nevertheless he said, "Sure, I'll ride with you."

He stepped into the saddle and walked his roan up beside Dantley's horse and they rode westward. Crabtree noticed that the sheriff kept glancing across his shoulder, looking to the south, toward Lookout Mountain. But he said nothing and they rode at an easy pace through the gray day, Sheriff Dantley whistling a little tune Crabtree had only heard once before— Shelter Morgan had been whistling the same tune the night before.

It was mid-afternoon before Shelter reached Lookout. He slowly circled the foot of the northern face, searching for tracks, finding none. Once, far off, he thought he heard a horse nicker, but through the wind it was difficult to be sure.

He found the road Gray had cut across the flats—the road which Jethro Partridge had used, which Gray's booty wagons used, and he turned up it, riding carefully, his rifle across the saddle bows.

In the gray light of day his logic was not so convincing. He really had no reason for believing Gray was up there, but believe it he did. Not with his reasoning faculties, but in his guts.

That knowledge sat there like an indigestible mass of hope, fear, exultation. Shelter rode higher, the wind sharp against his back, tiny wind-driven drops of rain peppering his cheeks and hands.

When he reached the point where Jethro had forced them into the tunnel, he pulled up, unsaddled the bay and tethered it near the wagons which sat hunched in the rain, their loads of ancient armaments returning to rust.

Shelter searched the area carefully, but the bootprints were smeared, unidentifiable. They could have been Jethros', Lavelle's or his own tracks. He stepped inside the tunnel and paused, listening to the wind rattle in the honeycomb of passageways. He listened, letting his eyes grow used to the darkness, and his patience was rewarded.

It came from deep within the massive tomb. A small sound, echoing and re-echoing down the cold stone chambers. A small sound, but a distinctive one. The sound of metal against stone.

Shelter spared a meager smile and moved ahead, creeping through the tunnel until he came to the spot where he had made his escape from Lavelle. There he was rewarded with a lantern which lay on the floor, unlighted, the coal oil half spilled out. He picked it up and hooked it on his belt in back, not wanting the light until it became necessary.

Now he moved by touch through the blackness of the caverns. He knew his way, or so he thought, but twice he got lost trying to retrace the route he and Violet had used the last time. Once it was necessary to light the lantern.

It flickered brightly, casting spectres of shadows against the stone, and when Shelter turned it off his eyes still made reddish-yellow spots against the darkness.

He moved with infinite caution, with intense patience. His boots whispered against the stone and every ten steps he forced himself to pause, to listen, to sniff the air.

Only the gun in his hand separated Shelter Morgan from some Neanderthal forbear who had crept through other frozen caves, not knowing which cavern held the yellow eyes, the slashing claws of the sabertooth.

His patience was rewarded. The sound came again, and it was nearer. Off down a shaft Shelter had not explored the chink of stone against metal — unmistakable, clearer and closer.

He thought of the Witch Woman, but he doubted she had returned to the mountain. There was only one logical identification. Benton Gray had to be there, at the end of that shaft.

The darkness was impenetrable now, and Shelter elected reluctantly to strike a match. It flared up briefly and his eyes greedily took in the lay of the shaft. He waved the match out quickly. The clinking subsided and Shelter crouched, holding his breath.

The light could have been seen, although he doubted it, assuming that the man was not working in the dark, he figured he would see Gray's light before Gray saw his.

But the sulphur from the match was distinct in the air, maybe the scent of it had wafted down to Gray. He crouched, drew back the cold hammer of his rifle and waited; after a time the clinking began again and he crept forward.

By the matchlight he had seen that the shaft dropped off steeply and he eased forward, expecting it when the floor of the tunnel fell sharply away. Dropping down twenty feet or so he reached a flat, hat-sized platform. From there the tunnel took off in two directions.

He paused, waited what seemed an interminable period of time, and then heard his leading sound again. He had taken six steps when he saw light.

Shelter froze. The thin shaft of light painted a narrow swatch of orange against the stone. The sound which had been methodical stopped again and Shelter felt his heart race a little. He took another cautious step and the light was snuffed out.

He was there. Benton Gray was there, and he knew.

Shelter examined his position on that narrow path, surrounded by stone walls, and he found it lacking. Yet there was no turning back now. He moved his boot slowly forward. A trickle of stone fell away and Shelter cursed silently.

One more step and then another. He could feel a warm draft of wind now, as if there had been a fire in the chamber ahead of him. One more step and the gun fired.

The muzzle flash was bewilderingly bright

in the darkness. The bullet slapped off the stone at Shelter's shoulder, the booming of the shot was loud in his ears. He went to a knee, desperate, angry, for by the crimson glare of the muzzle flash he had seen a face. Shadowed, painted with gunpowder fire, it was the face of Benton Gray.

As he went down Shelter levered through four shots from his rifle, spraying the interior of the cavern with singing lead.

Gray would have to fall back from that barrage of bullets and so Shelter pressed onward. Not cautiously now, but with reckless abandon. He charged the dark interior of the cave, firing twice more before he discarded the rifle and drew his Colt, rolling into the cave where his last bullet's ricochet was only now dying down.

He hit cold stone, rolled and came to a complete halt, flat on his belly, unmoving in the darkness. The Colt was before him, in both hands. He strained against the darkness, seeing nothing, hearing nothing.

He held perfectly still, strangling off his own breath. His heart pumped surging blood through his arteries. The stone beneath him was icy, the sweat on his face hot against cool skin.

The air was dusty, faintly smoky, motionless. Somewhere in the darkness a man waited, another man as still and as deadly as Shelter Morgan. They waited, their hearts thumping crazily in the sepulchre of stone. Lookout would be a tomb for one more man on this day.

Shelter's muscles cramped, knotted and his fingers felt wooden. He worked them slightly, feeling the cold, ready trigger beneath his index finger.

The room exploded with sound and light and rolling smoke.

Gray had leaped up and he fired five shots, scattering them around the room as he bolted, tipping over a rough table, his legs striding toward an unseen corridor.

Shelter fired back, cursed himself for missing and leaped to his feet, the red glow of the shots lingering in his vision.

He stumbled over an unseen object, felt for the corridor and thrust his Colt into it, blindly firing three times.

Punching out the spent cartridges, Shelter reloaded by feel, hearing the tinkle of brass casings against the stone. He fired again into the tunnel and dove into it, almost immediately losing his feet as the floor dropped away.

The memory of Violet falling into a shaft was brilliant in Shelter's mind. As soon as he felt his feet go, he lunged desperately out, gripping the lip of the shaft. He cursed himself for underestimating Benton Gray. The escape route had included a pit for any pursuers to fall into!

Rock fell away, bounding off the stone walls of the shaft and Shelter clawed his way out, knowing how close he had come to the end.

He lay shakily against the stone, surprised

and pleased to find the Colt still glued to his fingers. Some instinct had urged him to maintain his grip on the pistol even while he tumbled awkwardly through space.

He lay still a long moment, hoping that Gray would believe he had dropped into the shaft. But Gray did not return. Shelter got to hands and knees and then to a crouch, listening.

He heard the sound of boot leather on stone, far distant, and he rose, moving frantically down the dark, unfamiliar corridor.

He struck another match, expecting the explosion of gunfire, but there was none. The trail was narrow along a ledge which dropped off some fifty feet to a cavern floor below and then up along a water-filmed chute to the left.

Shelter eased ahead, pressing his chest to the wall, holding his Colt forward. He found another narrow landing after making the bend, a second tunnel, and following it, a window out into the brilliant world of daylight and fresh air.

Great clouds drifted past, imperturbable, thunder-laden. Shelter inched forward. There was no doubt in his mind that Gray would be waiting, wanting to take Shell as he eased out into the open air.

Emerging from the tunnel he would be an easy target. There was nothing else to do, however, but to retrace the long route down, and so Shell paused, thinking about it.

He unstrapped the lantern and set it aside. He wiped back his hair and took in deep gratifying breaths of cold air. *Up.* The man would be up above him, firing down.

There was a narrow ledge outside the cave window. Perhaps it had been a cannon emplacement during the long war. The stone was blackened as if by black powder.

He could see nothing of what lay on either side of the exit, above or below. He waited a while longer, wating Gray to grow uneasy, perhaps to figure Shelter had gotten lost or fallen into the trap.

Finally Shelter ran out of reasons for waiting—except for wanting to live. He checked out his Colt for the third time, took in a deep last breath and plunged out of the dark, cold cavern into the gray light of day.

Outside it was a world of jumbled clouds, rumbling thunder and arcing blue lightning. The thunder roared in Shelter's ears and the lightning flashed twice, three times, four.

Rock splinters slashed at his flesh and the thunder of his own echoed across the skies. Gray had been above him, firing down over an outcropping of blue stone. Shelter had been exposed for his shots, but firing down as he was Gray fired high. Still the bullets were near enough to make Shelter's body curl up at all the corners.

He had burst from the cave, rolled and desperately taken in the setting. Knowing that for Gray to take this exit there had to be some sort of trail, he searched for and found, in microseconds, the narrow beginning of a steep path.

Shelter heard the bullets impact, saw Gray's twisted face, felt the sting of stone fragments, and not certain if he had been hit or not, Shelter had fired back, seeing Gray's body jerk back before Shelter hurled himself headlong toward the trail beyond the ledge and the scant shelter of a surrounding stack of boulders.

He lay there gasping for breath. From nearby, thunder rumbled like an echoing of their shots. Glancing down, Shell saw that the earth fell away for a thousand feet or more.

His glance shuttled up the nearby path which was only a narrow groove cut by nature into the face of Lookout, and then to the spot where Gray had been.

Nothing moved but the constantly changing clouds. A draft of hard wind sprayed Shelter with brief rain. Lightning struck against the cloud-shrouded verdant valley below and a moment later a clap of ear-shattering thunder ruumbled.

Then it trickled down. Shelter saw it fall, saw it splat against the grey stone of the ledge. A drop fell and then another. Red blood staining the stone before the rain could wash it away.

Gray was hit then. How badly he could not tell. Was he still there, waiting? Again, no way of knowing. But the blood still trickled, perhaps from his living flesh, perhaps spilling from a pool of cold blood Gray had left behind.

Shelter moved to the upward-snaking path

and crept up, his face and hands against the rough stone, his Colt before him, always before him.

Nearer. He crept nearer the ledge where Benton Gray had waited. His hand found a level spot and he eased up slowly.

The gun exploded nearly in Shelter's face and he felt the white heat of pain in his chest. Thunder exploded across the skies and Shelter's mouth sagged open in an anguished scream of anger and pain. The rain swept down; dizziness swarmed over his blood-tangled thoughts.

He fired back, crawling up onto the ledge shakily, hair in his eyes, rain tacking his shirt to him. He saw Gray scrambling over a higher outcropping, dragging a leg, and he fired from his knees. Three times, one of the bullets nailing Gray to the stone. But the man crawled on, and Shelter reloaded, staggering to his feet, his eyes blurred with rain and pain, his chest and shoulder on fire as his own blood leaked out, staining his tattered shirt to running crimson.

He ran to the wall, legs wobbling crazily, thinking only of getting Gray, getting him before the life leaked out of his own shattered body.

He crawled upward, his right arm practically useless, the storm driving down against him. The smear of Gray's blood was on the stone, and Shelter's own blood merged with it as he crawled upward.

Here they would die—death's ironic little

joke. The two old warriors returning to the battlefield to die, their reprieve ended.

Shelter struggled upward, nearly losing his grip. Desperately he looked over his shoulder at the limitless space below, having a fleeting recollection of Jethro wheeling through space, his face already dead.

He clambered upward, rock tearing at his arms, his knees, and then he was up and over, onto the flat wind washed pinnacle of Lookout Mountain.

The man was there.

Benton Gray in a torn brown jacket, black pants and brown boots, his gun dangling in his white fingers as he watched, as he waited.

"Damn you," he breathed. "All this time. Couldn't you have left it alone?"

"You killed my men," Shelter panted. He walked toward Gray, pausing ten feet away.

"We could have talked!" Gray said in exasperation. Rain combed his long, thinning hair down across his eyes. A puddle of blood spread out beside his boot. He was dead on his feet, and he knew it. "I had it all, Morgan. You could have had some of it."

"I've got all of you I want, Gray. Your blood."

"It's no good . . . we'll both die. We could both live." His face was pallid, eyes bright, his teeth worked one row against the other. He shivered before the wind.

"If that's the choice, let's have at it," Shelter said bitterly.

"It's so important that I die?" he asked weakly.

Shelter nodded. "It is."

"Morgan . . ." whatever he was going to say, he never finished it. His mind had been decided. Shelter saw it, saw it in the shift of his eyes, the set of his jaw, the tensing of the cords in the throat, and when Benton Gray swung his gun up, Shelter was just an instant quicker.

Gray's bullet tugged at Shelter's shirt and the Colt in Shell's hand bucked. Twice, three times. Gray jerked like a crazed marionette, staggered and toppled back, his arms bent crazily, his heart stopped.

Shelter moved forward, the blood hot against his chest, the rain cold in his face. He stood over Benton Gray a long while, watching as the rain swept the blood away, cleansing Lookout Mountain, watching as the storm clouds rattled electric sabers and the wind chanted death songs to the silent earth.

13.

The bandage was tight and the new scab underneath itched like the devil, but the sun was warm, the sound the insects made in the brush pleasant, the gentle motion of the raft soothing.

Much more soothing was the sun-warmed woman flesh on top of Shelter Morgan. He opened his eyes and squinted into the sun at Violet.

"A little more, please," he said.

"You've got all there is," she answered with a sun-dazed smile.

Shelter lay on his back against the raft which was tied to the trunk of an ancient elm in this secluded bend of the lazy river. She was astride him, her lush thighs warm against his. He was buried in her depths, snug and warm, too lazily comfortable to move again.

Her breasts and shoulders were pinkened by the sun. Her nose was splashed with fresh, sun-sketched freckles. Her hands moved relentlessly, soothingly across his stomach and chest, returning life to his broken body, bringing warm blood back into flesh which had been terminally frozen, rain-washed, wind dried and bruised.

"Is it living up to expectation?" Shelter asked lazily. "You've waited a long time for this little voyage."

"It's everything that it could be," Violet answered.

She was beautiful, Shelter decided. She pooched out her lower lip and blew a strand of dark hair off her nose. Behind her the sunlight sparkled through the trees, painting a moving picture of winking sunshine and shadow.

He had been a week abed, feverish and weak as a kitten, half out of his head most of the time. Violet had determinedly nursed him back to health, pulling him back from the edge of death.

"I saw Duncan Corbett in Whynot," Violet told him.

"And how is Cousin Corbett?" Shelter asked from behind closed eyes. Violey swayed gently against him and he felt a rising need pushing lazy disinterest aside.

"Shame-faced. He couldn't look me in the eye. He said to apologize to you, Shelter. Said he's goin' to learn to do his own thinkin' from now on—away from the hills."

He was silent, the sun pressing against him like a soothing blanket. The current rocked the raft as gently as a baby's cradle.

"It took this to end all the feuding," Violet added. "You, Senator Gray."

"It could have been ended long ago, hundreds of years ago."

"That's what Pa said," Violet answered, her hands slipping across the hard muscles of his abdomen. "But he also said you understand why it never did stop. Says you know something of blood grudges."

Well, that was probably true, but phrasing it that way made Shelter uncomfortable. He had simply set out to administer rough justice where the law could do nothing. Benton Gray, all those who had come before—and would come—were brutal men, the kind who had put themselves above the law, above moral decency.

Shelter yawned and Violet peered at him, her deep blue-violet eyes wide and laughing. "Am I putting you to sleep? Want me to stop?"

"Don't stop anything you're doing," Shelter said. "What have we got planned for today?

Oh, yes. Drift down the river. Have lunch, make love in the sunshine and drift on. Very tiring work," he said.

"I've noticed you are tiring a little," she teased.

Shelter opened one eye and grinned. "I am only human."

"This morning I didn't think so." She was silent a moment. "Did I tell you that Polly Partridge is going to marry Sheriff Dantley?"

"Twice."

"Oh? It's a nice idea, hm?"

"Nice for Polly, nice for Dantley."

Violet was silent then; pouting a little she stopped kneading Shelter's flesh. Then he felt her hair brush his chest, her breasts sway across his flesh, her warm lips searching his mouth.

"Let's eat," she whispered, biting a little harder than was necessary on his ear lobe. "Keep up your strength."

They staggered onto the grassy clearing ashore, their bodies drained by love, the lazy heat of the day, and Violet opened the wicker picnic basket she had packed.

They ate thick ham sandwiches and fried chicken, washed down with lemonade which had been left to cool in the river. They stuffed themselves with fresh, yeasty biscuits smothered in butter and honey and finished with blueberry tarts made that morning.

Sagging back against the deep grass, sated, sleepy with the sun and the meal, they made love. Violet lay on her stomach against the grass and Shelter slid into her, spreading her with his fingers, finding her dewy, warm, ready.

He entered her and lay atop her, their warm flesh pressed together. Violet's head was turned to one side, pillowed on her forearms. Her eyelids flickered and she wriggled her hips with satisfaction.

A soft breeze floated across the lazy river, bringing scents of sweet grass, lush vegetation, earth and water. Shelter got to his knees and raised her hips to his pelvis, drawing her to her knees. Then he slowly stroked against her, watching the reaction on her drowsy face, the sweet soft cleft of her enveloping him until he shuddered and came, falling with her into the deep, spring scented grass.

Violet turned toward him, slung a leg over his hips and snuggled closer, her hair soft against his cheek. Shelter watched her doze, running an amazed hand along the curve of her hips, touching every angle and rising curve of her while she purred in her half-sleep.

The shadow which fell across them baffled his comfort-sluggish mind and he struggled with an elusive thought for a moment before his eyes came wide open and he turned sharply, letting Violet's startled head drop.

"A little picnic, huh?" Lavelle Partridge said maliciously, "Cozy, ain't it. All isolated like this." He looked around at the empty woods, the silent silver river.

"What do you want?" Violet said, coming to her feet, hands on hips, anger sparking in her eyes.

"Later," he said suggestively, "maybe you." Lavelle's dirty eyes swept over the lush lines of Violet Plank's body. "Fer now. I want him."

He lashed out with a boot and the breath rushed from Shelter's lungs in a painful gasp.

"It's all over, Lavelle," Shelter said, coming to his knees. "The feuding, all of it."

"Not for me." He stroked the scattergun he had cradled in his arms. "You whipped me, Morgan. Only man who ever done that. I didn't like the feeling, didn't like it at all, Cousin Morgan."

"He's in no shape to fight you, Lavelle!" Violet protested.

"Fight. I don't want to fight him, girlie. I want to kill him."

He stepped back, swinging the muzzle of that shotgun toward Shelter. Then he took another step back, saying, "I remember that trick you done me with last time. This time I won't be careless. Why don't you just rise on up to your feet, Cousin Morgan. Amble on down to the river."

Shelter rose, standing naked before the twin muzzles of Lavelle Partridge's scattergun. Twin eyes as black and cold as the eyes in Lavelle's head, eyes where savage intelligence flickered dully.

"Move on ahead now, Morgan," Lavelle said, "and don't worry about the little girl. I'll be back presently to finish her up real good."

Shelter hesitated and then turned his back. Wild thoughts collided in his mind. His only chance was to run, and that was no chance at all. The grass was prickly underfoot, the river shimmering like a mirror.

He heard a hammer being drawn back and then the awful roar of a gun. Shelter flinched but felt no pain. Smoke rolled across the clearing and he cautiously turned his head.

Violet stood there, her hands trembling, his Colt in her hands. Lavelle was dead against the grass, his cruel face slack in death. Shelter turned and walked to Violet. Her lips trembled and she lowered the gun.

"I put it in the picnic basket. I don't really know what made me do it."

"I'm just glad you did, damned glad."

He took her into his arms and she stood trembling for a time, tears running warm against Shelter's bare chest.

She sniffed, "I ought to keep hold of the damned thing, hold it on you till you marry me." She laughed, a sobbing, gasping little laugh. "But I guess that wouldn't be fair."

Violet stepped back, rubbing the tears from her cheeks with the back of her hand. She sniffled again and then found a smile.

"What now?" she asked.

"What now?" Shelter grinned. He nodded toward the raft which bobbed on the lazy surface of the lazy river. "Sail on, Captain. Sail on."

SPECTACULAR SERIES

READ THESE HORRIFYING BEST SELLERS!

THE NEST (662, $2.50)
by Gregory A. Douglas
An ordinary garbage dump in a small quiet town becomes the site
of incredible horror when a change in poison control causes huge
mutant creatures to leave their nest in search of human flesh.

CHERRON (700, $2.50)
by Sharon Combes
A young girl, taunted and teased for her physical imperfections,
uses her telekinetic powers to wreak bloody vengeance on her
tormentors—body and soul!

LONG NIGHT (515, $2.25)
by P. B. Gallagher
An innocent relationship turns into a horrifying nightmare of terror when a beautiful young woman falls victim to a man seeking
revenge for his father's death.

CALY (624, $2.50)
by Sharon Combes
When Ian Donovan and Caly St. John arrive at the eerie Simpson
House in Maine, they open a door and release a ghost woman
who leads them beyond terror and toward the most gruesome,
grisly experience that anyone could ever imagine.

THE SIN (479, $2.50)
by Robert Vaughan
A small town becomes the victim of a young woman's strange
sensual powers leading to unnatural deaths.

*Available wherever paperbacks are sold, or order direct from the
Publilsher. Send cover price plus 50¢ per copy for mailing and
handling to Zebra Books, 21 East 40th Street, New York, N.Y.
10016. DO NOT SEND CASH!*